MAN
AND
NIGHT

Mandie® Mysteries

MANDIE®
AND THE
NIGHT THIEF

Lois Gladys Leppard

BETHANY HOUSE PUBLISHERS
MINNEAPOLIS, MINNESOTA 55438

Mandie and the Night Thief
Copyright © 2003
Lois Gladys Leppard

MANDIE® and SNOWBALL® are registered trademarks
of Lois Gladys Leppard.

Cover illustration by Chris Dyrud
Cover design by Eric Walljasper

Published by Bethany House Publishers
11400 Hampshire Avenue South
Bloomington, Minnesota 55438
www.bethanyhouse.com

Bethany House Publishers is a Division of
Baker Book House Company, Grand Rapids, Michigan.

Printed in the United States of America

ISBN 0-7642-2640-1

This book is especially for
all those readers whose replies
to the questionnaire in
Book #35, *Mandie and the Quilt Mystery,*
were too late to win.

About the Author

LOIS GLADYS LEPPARD worked in Federal Intelligence for thirteen years in various countries around the world. She now makes her home in South Carolina.

The stories of her mother's childhood as an orphan in western North Carolina are the basis for many of the incidents incorporated into this series.

Contents

And forgive us our debts, as we forgive our debtors (Matthew 6:12).

Chapter 1 / An Unexpected Letter

Rain traveled with the train all the way home to Franklin, North Carolina, from New York. The windows had to be kept closed, and the air was warm and stale. Mandie and her friends kept wiping moisture off the glass, trying to see outside. A heavy downpour had started before they had boarded the train in New York.

"Oh, shucks!" Mandie said, giving a quick swipe to the window glass. "I can't see a thing. I'll never know what we've been through."

"But we've been to New York before," Celia reminded her.

"But most of our journey that time was in the dark," Mandie replied.

"I'm just thankful Jonathan's father was able to get this private car for us," Joe said.

Mandie glanced toward the adults sitting at the other end of the car. "That was an interesting argument between my grandmother and your father, Jonathan," she said.

Jonathan grinned at her and replied, "Your grandmother may own that ship line, but when it comes to trains my father is the winner. He never travels in an ordinary train car. He always has a private one."

"I'm glad we found out their secret while we were all at your house," Mandie told Jonathan.

"Yes," Jonathan agreed. "Otherwise we would never be making this trip together."

"We are only going to spend one night at your house, aren't we, Mandie, before we go on to Charleston?" Celia asked.

"That's what everyone agreed to," Mandie replied, sitting down in the seat by the window she had been wiping. "However, if Senator Morton is not at our house when we get there, we'll have to wait for him." She looked at Celia, who sat down next to her.

Joe and Jonathan flipped the back of the next seat so it was facing the girls and then sat down.

"Mandie, I just thought of something else," Celia said, turning to look at her. "Since Polly's mother didn't allow Polly to go to New York with our mothers, she is probably home and will be right over as soon as we walk in your door."

"Polly Cornwallis is not going with us to Charleston. I'll see to that," Mandie said firmly.

"Too bad she lives right next door to you," Jonathan remarked, "where she can keep up with your goings and comings."

The train went around a sharp curve. Everyone slid around in their seats.

"We certainly went around that curve in a hurry," Joe remarked.

"We feel it more than the other cars because we are on the end," Jonathan said.

Mandie glanced at her grandmother, sitting at the far end. "It didn't seem to bother Grandmother," she said. Mandie's white cat came from under her seat and jumped up into her lap. "Snowball, that must have shaken you awake." She rubbed the cat's head, and he meowed his thanks as he curled up.

"I suppose you are taking that cat with you to Charleston," Joe said.

"Of course," Mandie replied. "Snowball goes wherever I go. You know that." She grinned at Joe.

"Yes, I know that very well. All the escapades he has been involved in would make a book." He grinned back at Mandie.

"A book?" Mandie said, frowning as she thought about it. "Maybe I will write a book about Snowball."

"Mandie, it would never end because it just goes on and on, with Snowball into everything and anything," Celia remarked.

"All right, then. I could just call it *The Endless Book of Snowball's Adventures*. And that way I could keep adding on," Mandie replied with a laugh.

"I'm afraid no one would want to read it if it never ended, because every book has an ending," Jonathan said.

"And I hope this train ride has an ending soon," Joe remarked.

"You are in a hurry to get on down to Charleston, aren't you?" Mandie asked.

"Yes, and then on back home so I can have some time to spend with my parents before I have to go back to school," Joe told her.

"This is the first time my father has ever taken time off from work to go anywhere with me, and I am so grateful to be with him after all those boarding schools I have been sent off to," Jonathan said.

"And I've often thought it would be wonderful to be able to go to school near my home and not have

to go off to Asheville to the Heathwoods' school,"
Celia said.

"I have, too," Mandie said. "But my mother
wanted me to go to the Heathwoods' school because
she went there, and she considers it the best educa-
tion anywhere in the south." Looking at Celia sitting
next to her, she added, "And now when we finish
there next spring we'll have to go on to college."

"You girls should come on down to my college in
New Orleans and study there," Joe said.

"No, you should come to New York for college.
We've got lots of good schools," Jonathan said.
"And I don't intend leaving New York to go to col-
lege, either."

"But you have all those colleges to choose from.
Down in North Carolina where we live there aren't
any schools where I can meet the entrance require-
ments to study law," Joe said. "Therefore, I have to
go away to New Orleans where they allow me to
catch up, but I shall return," he finished with a big
grin as he raised his fist and shook it.

"I would like to go to college in Richmond so I
could stay home. We are only a few miles out of
town," Celia said.

Mandie quickly looked at her friend and said,
"But, Celia, you said if we decided to go to college
in Richmond we could live in the school even though
your home is near there."

Celia looked at Mandie, smiled, and replied, "If
you decide to go to college in Richmond, we could
both live at my home, instead of in the school."

Mandie thought about that for a moment and
replied, "I don't know about that, Celia. Your mother
might not want to put up with me."

"I'm sure she would be delighted to have you.

You could always bring Snowball with you, whereas in a college I'm pretty sure they won't allow the cat," Celia said.

The four young people finally became quiet and dozed in their seats. The journey from New York had been long and tiresome with rain beating against the windows of the train.

Mandie woke as the train gave a sudden lurch and came to a screeching halt. She grabbed the armrest and sat up to look out the window. She could see the sign "Franklin, North Carolina" hanging over the platform. Excitedly she told her friends, "Wake up, everybody. We're home!"

Her friends quickly straightened up, rubbed their eyes, and gazed out the window. Mrs. Taft had risen from her seat and was saying, "Gather up your belongings, you young people, and, Amanda, please don't let that cat get loose."

Mandie and her friends looked at each other as they stood up and smiled. Mrs. Taft always had to be in charge.

"Yes, ma'am," the four chorused as they picked up their bags and Mandie held tightly to Snowball.

As the young people followed the adults down the aisle toward the door, Mandie bent to look out the window. "I see Mr. Jason and Abraham out there," she told her friends.

"And I don't believe it's raining here," Joe said with a big grin.

Mrs. Taft led the way with Celia's mother, Jane Hamilton, right behind her and Jonathan's father, Lindall Guyer, carrying handbags. Mandie's mother, Elizabeth Shaw, and Mandie's uncle, John Shaw, who was married to Elizabeth, paused as they came up to the young people in the aisle.

"Be sure you have everything, Amanda," Elizabeth said.

"Yes, because this train is running late and it will be turning around and getting out of Franklin before you can say 'scat,' " John Shaw added with a big grin.

"Scat!" all four young people shouted.

"Now look at what y'all have done," John Shaw said, pretending to frown. "You've proved me wrong."

Mandie and her friends laughed as they followed the adults out of the train.

Jason Bond, who was John Shaw's caretaker, was waiting with the rig. He came forward to meet them. "Y'all brought the sunshine," he was telling John Shaw as he began taking their bags.

"Oh, Mr. Jason, it rained all the way from New York," Mandie said with a frown.

"Has Senator Morton arrived yet?" John Shaw asked Jason Bond as they walked on toward the rig.

"Yes, sir, Mr. John. He got here last night," the caretaker said, placing bags in the rig.

"I'm glad he did, because that means we can go on to Charleston tomorrow," John Shaw said.

Mr. Bond looked back at Mandie and said, "And that Miss Polly next door has been asking me every day if y'all were coming home." He grinned.

"Oh, goodness, Mr. Jason, she will probably be at the house when we get there," Mandie said with a loud moan as she looked back at her friends.

"Oh no!" Joe replied.

"We're in for some fun," Jonathan said, grinning at Mandie.

The adults had stepped into the rig, and John Shaw turned back to say, "Come on, get in. I see

Abraham over there with the wagon. He'll get the trunks."

When they got to the Shaws' three-story house, Senator Morton was waiting in the parlor. The adults went in to greet him.

Mandie set Snowball down and said to her friends, "Come on, let's go see Aunt Lou." She led the way to the kitchen.

Mandie pushed open the kitchen door and found Aunt Lou, John Shaw's housekeeper, standing by the big iron cookstove, where she was stirring food in a large pot. When she saw Mandie, she put down the spoon, wiped her hands on her big white apron, and came to embrace the girl.

"My chile done got home," Aunt Lou was saying as she hugged Mandie. And then, looking at the others, she added, "And she done brought them special friends with huh, too." She walked over to give Celia, Jonathan, and Joe a little squeeze. "Happy to see y'all," she told them.

At that moment the back door opened and Liza, the young maid, danced into the room, grinning as she looked at Mandie. "Dat Miss Purty Thang next do', she done been over heah ev'ry day askin' when y'all comin' home, and I tells huh maybe y'all ain't gwine come home right now but she didn't believe a word I said."

Everyone laughed so much it was hard for Mandie to get her breath to greet Jenny, the cook, who came in behind Liza. "I hope you've got a chocolate cake baked," Mandie said.

"Why, in fact, we's got two chocolate cakes baked," Jenny replied, going to throw open the doors in the safe, showing the two cakes sitting inside.

Joe rushed to her side and asked, "Can we begin eating them now?"

"Yes, we're really starving," Jonathan added as he joined Joe.

Jenny looked at Aunt Lou, who told the young people, "Why, sho' nuff, y'all can eat cake right now, and we's got a pot o' coffee ready. Just sit down there at the table." She turned to the young maid and said, "Liza, git de cups and plates down."

As soon as Jenny had served the cake and Aunt Lou had poured the coffee, Elizabeth Shaw stuck her head inside the door. "Amanda, remember you will have to eat supper in about two hours." Then, turning to the servants, she told them, "I'm so glad to be home and get y'alls wonderful cooking. And, Aunt Lou, we will be leaving early tomorrow morning for Charleston."

"Tomorrow mawnin', Miz Lizbeth?" Aunt Lou replied. "Why, I was hopin' y'all would stay awhile befo' you gwine down to dat Charleston town. Y'all won't have time to git yo' breath by tomorrow mawnin'."

"We have to go on tomorrow because Jonathan's father is with us and he has to get back to New York and back to work in a few days," Elizabeth explained. "Then we'll be home for the rest of the summer."

"Rest of de summer ain't much left by den," Aunt Lou fussed as she poured another cup of coffee. "Miz Lizbeth, you be wantin' we should take coffee to de parlor now?"

"Yes, please do, Aunt Lou, and just a little sweetbread or something, not the chocolate cake. That's too rich for this time of day," Elizabeth replied as she left the room.

"Liza, set up a tray for the parlor," Aunt Lou said.

Liza danced around the room and replied, "Dat senit man, he been waitin' all afternoon fo' his coffee, want to drink it wid Miz Grandma, he say. So now Miz Grandma done got heah and he'll be wantin' coffee." She talked as she got the tray ready.

Mandie and her friends smiled and listened.

"I wonder what happened when your father walked in with my grandmother and the senator was waiting for her in the parlor," Mandie said, then started giggling and almost choked on her coffee.

"We should have stayed to watch," Jonathan said with a big grin.

"I wonder if your father and Senator Morton know each other," Joe said, taking a bite of his piece of chocolate cake.

"Or if Senator Morton knows about all that went on when they were young," Celia added.

"I'm not sure," Jonathan said, sipping his coffee. Then, turning to Mandie, he asked, "How long has your grandmother known Senator Morton?"

"Oh, goodness, for ages and ages," Mandie replied, wiping tears of laughter from her blue eyes. "In fact, Senator Morton was a friend of my Grandfather Taft, and you know he died years before I was ever born, as far as I know."

"Then they probably know each other, because my father also knew your grandfather," he told Mandie.

"I've been wondering if Grandmother would eventually marry Senator Morton, but now that she and your father have become friends again, I'm not sure what will happen," Mandie said.

"I'm sure there will be some interesting moments

on this journey to Charleston," Jonathan said, grinning.

Aunt Lou had been listening to the conversation and asked, "My chile, did you git dat mail off de front table dat came fo' you whilst y'all been gone?"

Mandie looked up from her coffee and asked, "I got a letter?"

"You sho' did," Aunt Lou said as Mandie quickly rose from the table.

"I never get any mail. I'll be right back," Mandie told her friends.

Mandie rushed down the long hallway to the table near the front door where her uncle's mail was always put. She looked in the silver basket sitting on it, and sure enough, she spotted an envelope addressed to Amanda Shaw. Snatching it up, she started back toward the kitchen as she examined it.

"From Lily Masterson!" she said in surprise as she read the return address. "And she's back in South Carolina."

She tore open the envelope and exclaimed as she entered the kitchen, "A letter from Lily Masterson!" She pulled a single sheet of paper out of the envelope and unfolded it as she sat down.

"Lily Masterson, the girl who was on the ship with us when we went to Europe?" Celia asked.

"The older girl with the little sister named Violet?" Jonathan asked.

"Yes, yes," Mandie said as she quickly scanned the note. Then, looking at her friends, she said, "She has come back home to Fountain Inn, South Carolina."

"Is Fountain Inn anywhere near Charleston?" Celia asked.

"Why, I don't really know. Seems like it's on the

way to Charleston," Mandie replied.

"Yes," Joe said. "It's not very far over the border into South Carolina from here. I've never been there, but I'm sure that's where it is."

Mandie was excited as she said, "I wonder if Mother would stop there on our way so we could visit Lily?"

"Mandie, we are going on the train," Jonathan reminded her. "You can't just stop the train and get off wherever you happen to want to go."

"But maybe the train goes through Fountain Inn," Joe suggested. "And if it does you could get off there."

"I've wondered whatever happened to Lily and her little sister," Celia said. "Remember her mother had died and her father was sending them to England to live with their aunt?"

"Yes," Mandie agreed. "I should have stayed in touch with her. But now that she has let me know they are back, maybe we could visit them. As soon as I get a chance I'll discuss this with my mother or Uncle John."

"Well, what did she have to say in the letter?" Celia asked.

Mandie held up the single sheet of paper and said, "Nothing much, just, 'We're back in Fountain Inn and if you and your friends are ever down this way please come to visit.' That's all she said."

"Then let's go visit," Jonathan said with a big grin.

"Would all of you want to visit her?" Mandie asked.

"Well, since I have never met her, I don't believe I do, especially since I will only be able to spend a day or two in Charleston and then must get back home," Joe said.

"I would like to if we can arrange it," Celia said.

"And so would I," Jonathan agreed.

"Then I'll talk to my mother," Mandie said. Then she quickly looked at her friends and added, "You know, Grandmother knows Lily, too. Remember how nice Grandmother was to Lily when her little sister got sick on the ship?"

"Maybe your grandmother could arrange all this for us?" Jonathan suggested.

"Yes," Mandie said with a big grin. "We definitely need Grandmother on our side for this."

She quickly tried to figure out how she could speak to Mrs. Taft without the other adults around. That was going to be hard to do since her grandmother had two interesting men following her around for this journey to Charleston. There must be a way. And she would find that way.

Chapter 2 / Spying

As soon as everyone had finished their coffee and cake in the kitchen, Mandie told her friends, "Let's go to the parlor and see what's happening in there." Looking at Jonathan she added, "You know, between my grandmother and your father and Senator Morton."

Jonathan grinned at her as he rose and said, "Yes, let's do go to the parlor."

When the four young people entered the parlor, Mrs. Taft was not there. Mandie glanced at her mother as they sat down across the room from the adults.

"Where is Grandmother?" she asked.

"Mother has gone to her room to rest until time for supper," Elizabeth replied.

"Oh, shucks!" Mandie said to her friends.

"Amanda, you need to repack your trunk tonight with clothes for Charleston because we will be departing early tomorrow morning," Elizabeth told her.

"You too, Celia," Jane Hamilton said to her daughter.

"I suppose that includes us, too," Jonathan said, looking at Joe.

Joe stood up and said, "And I think I'll go do that right now,"

Mandie glanced at Celia and said, "We might as well do ours, too."

"Yes," Celia agreed.

"Be sure y'all are back down here on time for supper," Elizabeth reminded them as they left the room. "Six o'clock sharp."

"Yes, ma'am," the group chorused.

Celia always shared Mandie's room when she came to visit. Her trunk was sitting beside Mandie's on the far side of the huge room. Snowball was curled up asleep in the middle of the big bed.

Mandie bent over her trunk and began removing the contents and hanging up her clothes. "I'm not taking as much to Charleston as I did to New York," she said. "I didn't even wear all the things I took to Jonathan's house." She went to the wardrobe with an armful of dresses.

"I'm not, either, but remember, Mandie, when you visited the Pattons before, you said they dressed for dinner every night," Celia reminded her. "Therefore, we will need some dresses for that."

Mandie paused to look at the clothes in her arms. "I think I could mix some blouses and skirts and cut down on some clothes that way. Like this white lacy blouse here." She pulled out a hanger from the stack. "I could wear this several times with different skirts, or I could wear this black skirt several times with different blouses." She looked at Celia and asked, "What do you think?"

"Yes, that would be a very good idea," Celia agreed. "And I'll do the same thing. And be sure to take lots of ribbons. Those will help change the looks of anything we wear twice." She lifted a pile of clothes from her trunk and laid them on the big bed to sort them.

Snowball woke up, stretched, and began washing his face.

There was a slight tap on the door and Liza stuck her head inside. "Dat Miz Purty Thang next do' be down in de parlor."

"Polly Cornwallis is in the parlor?" Mandie quickly asked.

"She sho' is," Liza replied. "And huh mother, she be wid huh."

Mandie blew out her breath and said, "Well, maybe she'll go back home with her mother. I hope she doesn't stay for supper."

"Nope, she ain't stayin' 'cuz dey got comp'ny comin', huh mother said," Liza explained.

"I'm glad to hear that," Mandie said as she continued hanging clothes in the wardrobe.

"Huh mother tol' yo' mother maybe dey come back later and yo' mother say y'all gwine bed early tonight 'cuz y'all be leavin' early tomorrow," Liza explained, grinning as she looked at the two girls.

"Maybe we won't have to see them, then," Mandie said to Celia. Then, turning to Liza, she said, "Would you please come back and let us know when they go home? We could just stay up here until time for supper."

"I sho' will," Liza said and went on down the hall.

The girls repacked their trunks and then cleaned up and changed clothes for supper. And Liza still had not come back to let them know Polly had gone home.

As Mandie finished brushing her long blond hair and tying it back with a red ribbon to match her calico dress, she said, "We will have to go down in a few minutes. Mother said six o'clock sharp for supper and it's five minutes till." She looked at the clock on the mantelpiece.

"Yes, and I'd rather not be late," Celia said, shaking out the folds of her long skirt before the full-length mirror in the corner.

There was a knock on the door, and Mandie opened it to find Joe and Jonathan outside.

"Y'all ready to go downstairs?" Joe asked.

Mandie looked back at Celia and said, "I suppose we'd better go now." Then, turning to the boys, she said, "Liza let us know Polly is in the parlor with her mother."

Mandie and Celia followed the boys down the hallway as they talked. "But she said they are going home when we have supper," Celia said.

"We don't have much time here at your house anyway," Joe reminded her. "Did you girls get everything repacked?" They went down the staircase.

"Yes, we did," Mandie replied. "And I believe we'll be leaving about daylight in the morning."

As they came to the parlor door, Mandie was relieved to see that Polly and her mother were not there. Liza came hurrying up behind them, stuck her head in the doorway, looked directly at Mandie's mother, and announced, "De food on de table, Miz Lizbeth."

"Thank you," Elizabeth replied and the adults all rose.

Turning to Mandie, Liza whispered, "Dat Miz Purty Thang, she dun went home jes' now wid her muther." She danced on down the hallway toward the kitchen.

The young people followed the adults into the

dining room. Mrs. Taft had been in the parlor, and Mandie tried to catch up with her as they walked along. However, Elizabeth kept up a steady stream of talk until they were all seated at the long table. The young people were placed together on one side of the huge dining table, so Mandie could not speak to her grandmother, who sat at the end of the other side. And Senator Morton sat directly across from Mrs. Taft. Mr. Guyer was placed next to Jane Hamilton.

Mandie whispered behind her hand to her friends, "I wonder who decided to put Mr. Guyer next to Celia's mother. Do y'all think they are interested in each other?"

Her friends all laughed, causing the adults to glance in their direction.

"Oh no, Mr. Guyer is too old for my mother," Celia quickly told them.

The young people laughed again. And Jonathan said, "My father and Celia's mother have been friends a long time, I believe."

"Senator Morton is certainly keeping his eyes on my grandmother," Mandie whispered. "And my grandmother is not exactly looking at anyone."

"Would you like for your grandmother to marry the senator or my father?" Jonathan asked Mandie, grinning at her.

Mandie blew out her breath and replied, "Neither one."

"Neither one?" Celia asked. "I thought you wanted your grandmother to marry Senator Morton and go to live with him down in Florida so she wouldn't be around watching us."

"Well, that was before I found out about Mr. Guyer and my grandmother," Mandie said, smiling at Jonathan. "I just couldn't decide which one I like better."

"I don't believe your grandmother is interested in my father anymore," Jonathan said. "After all, that was many years ago when they knew each other."

"You just don't want my grandmother for your stepmother," Mandie said with a giggle. "And I would agree with you."

Joe finally joined the conversation. "Mandie, I would say that none of us would have any say-so about it. After all, I know your grandmother very well and she is usually the boss," he said grinning.

Mandie straightened up in her chair, blew out her breath, and said, "You are absolutely right, Joe. So I'm going to mind my own business while we are in Charleston." She tried to look serious.

"I don't believe that," Joe said, laughing.

"And neither do I," Celia added with a big smile.

"I'll volunteer to help you with your snooping in Charleston," Jonathan said, grinning at Mandie.

"Just remember you said that, Jonathan Guyer," Mandie replied.

No one seemed to be in a hurry to finish the evening meal. Mandie kept hoping she would be able to speak to her grandmother about Lily's letter, but when the meal was finally finished everyone went back to the parlor for coffee.

"Do we have to go to the parlor, too?" Jonathan whispered to Mandie as they rose from the table.

"I suppose so. My mother didn't say," Mandie whispered back. "However, maybe we can find an excuse to get out of there before too long."

"The chocolate cake will probably be served in the parlor," Joe reminded the others as they followed the adults.

"As soon as we can eat the cake, then, let's try to slip out and go sit somewhere where we can talk without the grown-ups overhearing everything," Jonathan said.

They followed the adults back to the parlor and sat down at the end of the room. Cake and coffee were served and the young people hastily ate theirs.

Mandie looked at her friends and whispered, "Maybe we could leave now."

Before anyone could reply, Elizabeth spoke from across the room, "Amanda, you should prepare to retire for the night now. We will be up before daylight in the morning."

Mandie glanced at her friends and then said, "Yes, ma'am." She stood up and whispered to the others, "Let's go." Turning to look across the room, she said, "Good night, everyone."

As she left the parlor the others followed. She led the way down the main hallway to the back parlor, where one lamp was burning, and as soon as everyone had come into the room she softly closed the door.

"I would like to talk to my grandmother, but I haven't had a chance," Mandie said as she sat down on the settee and her friends found seats nearby.

"Couldn't you just tell her you want to talk to her?" Joe asked.

"And then everyone who heard me would wonder why I want to talk to her," Mandie said. "Or, knowing my grandmother, she might just ask out loud what it was about."

"You want to talk to her about Lily's letter, don't you?" Celia asked.

"Yes, I'm hoping she can figure out how we could visit Lily," Mandie replied.

"Maybe you could go to her room later tonight after everyone has retired," Jonathan suggested.

"If I can catch up with her," Mandie agreed. "But since she evidently had a nap in her room before supper tonight, she may stay up late."

"We can keep watch for her to leave the parlor and you could catch her on the way to her room," Celia said.

Mandie went over to the door and quietly opened it a little. "I think we will be able to hear her whenever she leaves the parlor because she has to come down this way to go up the stairs." She went back to sit on the settee.

"What if she sees us in the parlor here? Won't she wonder what we're doing since we were supposed to go to our rooms?" Joe asked.

"She won't be able to see us if we stay away from the doorway," Mandie replied.

The four young people sat quietly while they listened for the others to leave the front parlor. Time passed slowly and Mandie became impatient.

"I thought they would be going to bed early," Mandie whispered to her friends. "Shh!"

At that moment they heard voices in the hallway.

"That's my mother, Celia's mother, Uncle John, and Mr. Guyer," Mandie said to her friends. "But I don't hear Grandmother." She quickly went to peep through the small opening in the doorway. "And they're going up the steps."

As soon as the voices died away up the stairs, Jonathan said, "Your grandmother and Senator Morton must be still in the parlor."

"Yes, maybe they'll come out soon," Mandie replied.

The four young people waited and waited, and

nothing else happened. They were all beginning to get sleepy.

"Why don't we all go to our rooms, Mandie, and you could try catching your grandmother tomorrow morning," Joe suggested.

"I know we can't just sit here all night, but what in the world is my grandmother talking about all this time with Senator Morton?" Mandie said. She stood up and added, "I think I'll slip down the hallway and try to look into the parlor."

"Do you want me to come with you?" Celia asked.

Mandie paused at the door, looked back, and said, "If I'm caught I may be in trouble, Celia, and I wouldn't want you to get involved, too."

Jonathan quickly stood up and said, "I'll go with you. I won't be in trouble for staying up late if I'm caught, because we stay up all hours at home anyway."

Mandie shrugged her shoulders and said, "You can come if you want to, but don't blame me if anything goes wrong and we get in trouble." She pushed the door open enough to slip through into the hallway.

Jonathan came right behind her and together they quietly walked down the hall toward the parlor door. Just as they got there Mrs. Taft and Senator Morton came out.

"Amanda, I thought you went to your room," Mrs. Taft said, glancing at her and then at Jonathan.

Senator Morton stood by Mrs. Taft's side, listening to the conversation.

Mandie looked at the senator and then at her grandmother. "I had something I wanted to do before I went to bed."

"And so did we, dear. So much has happened since we last saw Senator Morton," Mrs. Taft replied, looking up at the tall man.

"Indeed it has," Senator Morton agreed. He laughed and added, "And we still haven't caught up with the latest."

"Now, Amanda, you should run along and do whatever it is that you wanted to do and then get some sleep. Otherwise you are going to be awfully sleepy tomorrow for our journey." She walked on down the hallway toward the staircase with Senator Morton following.

Mandie stood there with her mouth open and then said to Jonathan, "Now, why didn't I just ask her to talk with me a few minutes?"

Mandie and Jonathan watched as Mrs. Taft and Senator Morton went up the stairs.

"There's nothing left to do but what Joe suggested: Get up early tomorrow and catch her before breakfast," Jonathan told her.

"I suppose that's what I'll have to do," Mandie replied, blowing out her breath and walking back toward her friends.

Celia and Joe waited for them in the doorway.

"Grandmother and Senator Morton are catching up on news, or whatever," Mandie told her friends. "And I didn't say anything about talking to her." She went back into the back parlor and flopped on the settee. Her friends followed.

"I say we all go to our rooms and get some sleep," Joe said, walking about the room.

"Yes," Celia agreed.

"I suppose we had better," Mandie replied with a loud moan. She stood up.

"Shh!" Jonathan warned. "Someone's coming

down the staircase." He stood in the doorway and looked down the hall.

The others crowded behind him.

"Why, it's Liza," Mandie said as the girl came down the steps and into the hallway toward them.

When Liza saw them, she stopped and said, "Lawsy mercy, y'all s'posed to be in yo' beds sleeping. Now whut y'all a-doin' back heah?" She came to the doorway.

"We're going right now, Liza, but what are you doing yourself? Aren't you supposed to be in bed now?" Mandie asked.

"Aunt Lou, she say I should go and be sho' dem men didn't leave no pipe burnin' in de parlor," Liza explained. "And de doors all locked up."

"But that's Mr. Jason's job, isn't it, Liza?" Mandie asked.

"Dat Mistuh Jason ain't heah right now," Liza replied as she danced around the hallway. "He be gone to Asheville."

"To Asheville? What for, Liza?" Mandie asked.

"Mistuh John, he send a paper to his lawyer man in Asheville, I heard him say," Liza replied. "And Mistuh Jason, he won't be back till 'morrow." She came to a halt in front of Mandie and asked, "And whut y'all be doin' down heah at dis heah hour?"

"We were starting upstairs when we heard you, and we waited to see who it was," Mandie explained.

"I'se s'posed to come and wake y'all up at five o'clock in de mawnin'. Y'all ain't got long to sleep tonight," Liza said.

"All right, all right," Mandie said. "We're going now." She started toward the staircase and her friends followed. She stopped and looked back.

"Liza, where is Snowball? Have you seen him tonight?"

"I sho' has," Liza said with a big grin. "He's a smart cat. He done gone to bed on yo' bed. Now dat Miz Grandma, she ain't dat smart. She sittin' on de settee down de hall jes' a-talkin' up a blue streak to dat senit man."

The young people looked at each other. Mandie blew out her breath and said, "All right, she can just sit there all night. We're going to bed. Good night, Liza." She continued down the hallway and her friends followed.

Mandie muttered to her friends, "I wonder what she has found to talk so much about."

"She's probably making plans for everyone when we get to Charleston," Jonathan said as they continued up the staircase.

Mandie looked back and said, "If they're sitting on the settee at the other end of the hall, we won't be passing them, so we can't hear what they are saying."

"We shouldn't eavesdrop anyway, Mandie," Celia said close behind her.

"Yes, I know," Mandie agreed. "Well, anyhow, good night, Joe and Jonathan. We'll see you early in the morning." She stopped to open the door to her room as she glanced at Mrs. Taft and Senator Morton sitting at the far end of the hall.

Joe and Jonathan were sharing a room across the hall. Jonathan opened the door to their room and the boys went inside after saying good-night.

Mandie opened the door to her room and she and Celia hurried inside to get ready for bed.

"I'll try to catch Grandmother before breakfast," Mandie said as she began turning the covers on the bed down, causing Snowball to scramble up to the pillows. "And, Snowball, you are not sleeping on my pillow." She pushed him down to the foot of the bed.

Mandie stayed awake a long time after she and Celia went to bed, trying to figure out how she could catch Mrs. Taft alone. Maybe tomorrow morning she would go to Mrs. Taft's room before they went down to breakfast. That is, if she woke up in time.

Chapter 3 / Is There a Mystery?

Mandie felt as though she had just gone to bed when Liza came into her room, talking loudly as she drew back the draperies.

"Time to git up now," Liza was saying as Mandie tried to pull the covers over her head.

Celia sat up in the bed and yawned. Snowball opened one eye to look at her.

"Gotta git up now, right now," Liza told Mandie as she yanked the covers off her.

Mandie rubbed her eyes and slid out of bed. Celia followed.

"We just now went to bed," Mandie fussed as she stretched.

"I done tole y'all you have to git up at five o'clock," Liza said, pulling back the last curtain. "Now git yo' clothes on and git down to de dinin' room. Breakfast is already on the table."

Mandie looked at Liza and asked, "Is Grandmother already downstairs?"

"Ev'ybody done downstairs 'ceptin' y'all," Liza replied. "Now git a move on, 'cuz I has to stay heah and be sho' y'all git dressed. If you want any breakfast you bettuh hurry."

34

The girls quickly scrambled into their clothes, which they had hung out the night before and which they would be wearing on the train trip.

"I'm ready," Mandie said as she brushed her hair and tied it back with a ribbon.

"So am I," Celia said, tying the bow at the neck of her blouse.

"Den let's git movin'," Liza said as she opened the door. Snowball jumped off the bed and stretched on the floor.

When the girls got to the dining room, Liza gave them plates and they went to the buffet to get their food. Everyone else was already there and everyone seemed to be talking at one time.

"Grandmother is still talking," Mandie said to Celia as she glanced at Mrs. Taft sitting between Mr. Guyer and Senator Morton at the table.

"I'd say she is enjoying having the attention of two men at one time," Celia replied with a big grin.

"I agree," Mandie replied.

The girls filled their plates and went to sit with Joe and Jonathan at the table.

"Glad to see you girls finally made it," Jonathan teased as he took the last bite of food on his plate.

"We were afraid we would have to go without you all," Joe said with a big grin.

"We got up at five o'clock. Y'all must have stayed up all night to get down here so early," Mandie teased back, quickly drinking her coffee.

"We didn't stay up all night, but your grandmother might have. She's still talking," Jonathan said, rolling his eyes in the direction of Mrs. Taft. "You will probably never get a chance to talk to her."

"I'll figure out a way to talk to her sometime

before we start back home from Charleston," Mandie said firmly.

Everyone finally got ready and got down to the depot and into Mr. Guyer's special train car, which had been pulled over on a side rail waiting for them. The train came into the depot, coupled it up at the end, and they were on their way to Charleston.

The young people slept most of the way after not getting much rest the night before. Snowball had his own seat and only woke up to use his sandbox and nibble on food in his dish. The adults talked now and then and dozed in between.

Mandie was jerked awake by the train rounding a curve sharply. She looked out the window and became excited.

"Look!" she told her friends, who were also straightening up in their seats after the jolt. "There's the Spanish moss! We are getting close to Charleston now. See the swampland? We'll be in the city soon."

"I'm so glad we are almost there. This seat has not been comfortable to sleep in," Celia said with a frown.

As the buildings of the city came into view, Mrs. Taft rose and straightened her hat. Elizabeth sat up in her seat and looked out the window and then spoke to Mandie down the length of the car. "Amanda, get your things together now. And please hold on to that cat."

Jane Hamilton added, "And, Celia, please don't leave anything on here."

Lindall Guyer rose from his seat and said, "This car will be put on a sidetrack here and will be locked up until we are ready to go home, so if anyone does leave anything in here it will be safe."

"Thank you, Mr. Guyer, for bringing us in your special car," Mandie said as he came toward them and the door.

"Yes, sir, thank you," Joe added.

"And I thank you," Celia said.

"Not to be outdone by my friends, Dad, I am most grateful for this journey with you," Jonathan told his father.

Mr. Guyer stopped and looked at the young people. "After all these thanks, I hardly know what to say. Could it be that the group is hinting for something else special?" He grinned at them as he reached the door.

Two redcaps came into the car to take the luggage, and soon everyone was out on the platform, where Tommy Patton and his father waited for them.

After exchanging greetings, Mr. Patton told them, "We have the carriage here for the adults, and Tommy will take the young ones in the rig. Don't bother with luggage checked. My driver is waiting over there for the train to be unloaded, and he will bring it to the house."

Mandie and her friends quickly went over to the rig in the yard with Tommy. She held tightly to her white cat. "Do you really know how to drive this rig?" she asked teasingly.

Tommy grinned back at her and said, "Of course. Been driving it since I learned to ride a horse, and that was ages ago."

Mandie looked up into the rig as she started to step aboard. She paused, reached for Celia's hand behind her, and exclaimed, "Celia! Look who's here."

Robert, Celia's friend at Mr. Chadwick's School for Boys in Asheville, rose from a seat in the rig and jumped down and came to stand by Celia.

"Robert!" Celia exclaimed. "When did you get here?"

"I came home from school with Tommy," Robert explained, smiling down at Celia, "after I heard y'all were going to be here."

Celia looked up at the shy young man as he ran his fingers through his unruly brown curls and smiled shyly at her. "I'm so glad you did," she said.

Mandie looked at her friends and smiled. She knew Celia liked Robert a whole lot. And the feeling seemed to be mutual.

Tommy followed in the rig behind the carriage, and as they all pulled up through the gate before the Pattons' huge three-story mansion, Mandie felt as excited as she had been the other time she had been there to visit.

Mrs. Patton was waiting for them in the parlor and greetings were exchanged. All the adults had been friends for years and years.

Mandie looked around for Tommy's sister, Josephine, but did not see her anywhere. Turning to him she asked, "Where is Josephine?"

"Josephine is visiting some friends out at the beach this week. I'm not sure when she will be back," Tommy explained.

"I hope she didn't go away because we were coming," Mandie replied with a frown.

She and Josephine were certainly not friends. The girl was forever trying to stir up trouble when Mandie had visited before. Mandie was glad she was not home this time.

"I'm not sure she even knew y'all were coming," Tommy said. "This visit to her friends had been planned for a long time."

Mandie looked around the parlor. Everything was expensive and beautiful. She noticed Joe also gazing around the room. She leaned close to him and said, "It looks like a room out of a castle."

Joe muttered back, "Yes, even though I saw it before when you left from here to go to Europe, I have to gaze around."

Mandie leaned closer again as she sat next to him on the settee. "I'll take Charley Gap any day," she whispered.

Joe grinned at her and said, "So would I."

One of the servants came to let Mrs. Patton know the guests' luggage had been put in their rooms. Looking around the parlor Mrs. Patton said, "Now, if any of you would like to go to your rooms and freshen up, your things are already there. Let's meet in the drawing room at six o'clock before we go to supper."

The Pattons seemed to have an endless number of servants hovering around the hallway to take the guests to their rooms.

Mandie was delighted to find that she was being put in the same room she had used during her other visit. And Celia was sharing it with her.

"This is such a beautiful room," Mandie exclaimed as she and Celia were left alone in the room. "Everything in it is blue. Blue, blue, everywhere. And I like blue." She twirled around in the middle of the huge bedroom.

"Yes, it is a beautiful room, in case you like blue," Celia replied teasingly.

Mandie stopped to look at her friend. "You are excited because Robert is here, aren't you?"

Celia grinned as she plopped down into a chair and said, "Well, I suppose so, a little, anyhow." She jumped up and went to the wardrobe. "Now I have to find something to put on." The servants had already hung up their clothes.

"Yes, me too, and get rid of this traveling suit," Mandie said, beginning to shed her clothes as she followed Celia.

Snowball sat in the middle of the huge bed, washing his face and watching his mistress. Mandie glanced at her cat and said, "You know, Celia, I just remembered something. Mrs. Patton is allergic to cats, I believe."

"Oh dear!" Celia stopped to look at her as she replied, "What are you going to do with Snowball?"

"When we were here before I tried to keep him away from her, and Mr. Patton said it was all right if Snowball came with us to visit that time, so I suppose it is all right this time. I'll just have to watch Snowball and try to keep him away from her this time."

"I'll help you watch out for him," Celia promised.

"Will you also help me watch Grandmother? I hope she has a room near us on this floor," Mandie said, putting on a blue dress with white lace and ribbons on it. "I'd like to talk to her about Lily and get that settled."

"Yes, I will let you know if I find out where her room is," Celia replied. She smoothed down the skirt of the green dress she had put on. She turned in front of the full-length mirror and then asked, "Do I look all right?"

Mandie grinned and said, "You look fine, Celia, and I know Robert will think so, too."

"That was a big surprise, finding him here," Celia said, continuing to turn in front of the mirror.

"You know Tommy invited him here because of

you," Mandie said, adjusting the sash on her dress.

Celia stood still and looked at her. "But suppose I had not wanted him to come here?" she asked.

"Oh, Celia, anyone who has seen you and Robert in the same company could tell that y'all are attracted to each other," Mandie said. "Now come on. Let's go down to the drawing room a little early and see who's there." She started for the door. Looking back at Snowball asleep on her bed, she said, "I'm leaving him here for the time being."

Celia followed Mandie out into the hallway. "Don't walk so fast, Mandie. People will think we are in a big hurry to get back with the boys," she said.

Mandie slowed down a little and continued on her way to the huge staircase. Celia followed, looking all about as she went.

The boys were in the drawing room, but Mandie gazed about her as she entered. She had never seen such a luxurious room before. She remembered when she saw it for the first time on her previous visit to the Pattons. The furniture was upholstered in peach and gray silk brocade. The draperies were a darker shade of gray with gold tassels. The carpet, which covered most of the parqueted floor, was so thick she sank into it as she walked. And there was Melissa Patton's portrait hanging over the gray stone fireplace that covered almost an entire wall.

Tommy stood up and stepped forward as the girls looked at the portrait and said, "This is one of my father's grandmothers, remember, Mandie?"

"Oh yes, I remember, and I think she is so real-looking, as though she's about to speak," Mandie replied.

"She is so beautiful," Celia commented.

Robert joined them standing there in front of the

fireplace. "We came down early, hoping you girls would, also," he said.

Joe came to join them and said, "Well, I came down early hoping to find a little food somewhere." He grinned.

"We'll be going into the dining room in about a half hour, after all the others have joined us," Tommy told him.

Turning to Celia, Mandie said, "I hope my grandmother comes down before the others and that she is alone."

Jonathan overheard the remark and said, "I doubt that you will be able to get your grandmother alone for a single minute, with two admirers following her around." He grinned at Mandie.

"Admirers?" Tommy asked.

Mandie explained what had been going on, that Jonathan's father and Senator Morton both seemed interested in her grandmother. "And I've been trying to catch her alone to talk to her about Lily. Remember Lily that I met when we went to Europe? She is back home in Fountain Inn and I want to go visit her. Therefore I need my grandmother on my side when I approach my mother with this request."

"Is there anything I can do to help?" Tommy asked.

"No, not that I know of. Thanks anyway," Mandie replied.

"Let's sit down," Jonathan said.

The group moved across the room to two settees facing each other.

Soon thereafter the adults began coming into the drawing room. Mr. and Mrs. Patton were the first ones, and as soon as they sat down, Mandie's mother, Elizabeth, and Uncle John followed; then

Jane Hamilton came in with Lindall Guyer, and finally Mrs. Taft joined them with Senator Morton.

"I'd say your grandmother is awfully interested in the senator and is ignoring my father," Jonathan whispered to Mandie.

"Grandmother can be very misleading sometimes," Mandie whispered back. She watched as Mrs. Taft sat down near the fireplace and Senator Morton took a chair opposite her.

"Celia, it looks like my father and your mother are getting around together," Jonathan whispered to Celia.

Celia looked at her mother. She had sat down near Elizabeth, but Lindall Guyer had taken the chair next to her. Turning back to Jonathan, Celia said, "I don't want my mother to get interested in your father, Jonathan, because I certainly am not going to move to New York." She smiled.

"Oh, but your mother loves New York," Jonathan reminded her.

"This is all silly talk," Celia said. "Just because my mother sits next to your father or enters the room with him is not saying that they are anything but friends, and they have been friends for many years, remember." The smile faded off her face as she added, "Besides, my mother is still in love with my father even though he died a long time ago now."

The other young people were silent. Then Joe said, "I wonder if we'll have chocolate cake for dessert." He smiled at his friends.

"Joe Woodard, one of these days you are going to get fat, always eating chocolate cake," Mandie teased.

"We may be having coconut cake tonight,"

Tommy Patton told them. "That is my mother's favorite, and our cook can make the best I've ever had."

"Oh, let's talk about something other than food," Mandie said with a deep sigh. Looking at Tommy she asked, "Have you had any mysteries around this big house lately?"

"I knew it would be about mysteries," Joe said, pretending to be bored.

"I'm not sure it would be called a mystery, but we have heard on the third floor a couple of times what we thought might be squirrels, but no one has investigated," Tommy said.

Mandie immediately perked up. "Exactly what kind of noise was it? Was it inside the walls or closets, or what?"

"I'm sorry, but I don't know," Tommy said. "I just overheard Rouster telling the other servants about hearing something. So now the other servants won't go up on that floor alone. You know they're all suspicious of ghosts and things." He laughed.

"Maybe we could find out what it is," Mandie said, smiling at Tommy. "Why don't we go up there and look around?"

"Mandie!" Joe said.

"Well, we could go up there, but we probably wouldn't hear anything," Tommy said. "Rouster has been listening for it whenever he goes up on the third floor. But after those two times that he did hear it there hasn't been any more noise up there," Tommy explained.

Mandie leaned forward and said, "Couldn't we just go up and look around?"

"Now, why didn't I keep my mouth shut?"

Tommy said with a grin. "I should have known you'd build it into a mystery."

"But couldn't we just go up there?" Mandie insisted.

"Yes, but I don't know when we'll have the opportunity," Tommy replied. "I think my mother has lots of things planned to do while you all are here."

"All right, in between whatever she planned, then," Mandie said. "She can't have every minute filled up."

"All right," Tommy agreed. "We'll pick the right opportunity and go look."

"I knew you would agree," Mandie said. "Thank you, Tommy." She smiled at him.

"I hope we don't have to spend all our time listening for sounds in the walls," Joe said, blowing out his breath.

"We won't be doing that, because I believe my mother is planning on going out to Mossy Manor to stay part of the time y'all are here," Tommy said.

Mossy Manor was the Pattons' old plantation house that Mandie and the others had visited while they were in Charleston on another visit.

"Maybe we would be able to find out what the noise is before we go out there," Mandie said.

"Yes, let's work real fast and solve the mystery so we can do other things," Joe said with a big grin.

"Yes, we can do that," Mandie agreed. She was secretly wondering how she could get up to the third floor and look around. Surely she would have an opportunity to do so.

Chapter 4 / Secrets About Charleston

All during the evening meal Mandie tried to listen to the adults' conversation and carry on a conversation with her friends. She was anxious to know what everyone's plans were for the evening because she intended slipping away from her friends and going to investigate the third floor if she had an opportunity at all.

Also, she was trying to figure out exactly what her grandmother would be doing for the rest of the night, whether she would retire early or sit and talk with Mr. Guyer or Senator Morton. Mandie was hoping Mrs. Taft would be tired from their journey that day and would go to her room after supper.

Then she became aware of the conversation among her friends.

"What is on the third floor of this house? I mean, do y'all use that floor, too, just you and your mother and father?" Celia was asking.

"It is furnished, like the rest of the house, but we very seldom open it up. Sometimes we may have lots of guests overnight and we put them up there," Tommy replied.

Mandie smiled at him and asked, "You put your guests up there with this noise you told us about?"

"None of our guests have heard it that I know of. It was some of the servants, or I believe Rouster, who started this tale about the noise," Tommy replied.

"What did your parents say about it when Rouster told them?" Celia asked.

"Oh, they just laughed and said it was probably squirrels, and we do have lots of squirrels around here," Tommy said.

"So they didn't think it was important enough to investigate?" Joe asked.

"I don't suppose so. They haven't done anything about it that I know of," Tommy said.

"Well, then, there seems to be no problem," Robert added.

"But don't y'all want to know what made the noises right here in your own house?" Mandie asked Tommy.

"It doesn't bother me. It's the servants who are making such a big to-do about it," Tommy said as he drank his coffee.

"Well," was all Mandie could think of to say to that. However, she was secretly thinking she would investigate on her own if no one cared to go up there with her.

"Are y'all interested in going out to our beach house for a day or two?" Tommy asked.

"Oh yes, I'd like that," Joe said. "You know we don't have an ocean back home in North Carolina."

"Yes, that would be nice if I don't have to stay out in the sun there, because you know with my red hair I freckle awful in the sunshine," Celia said, pushing back her long curly hair.

"You could just come out on the beach after the

sun goes down," Robert teased her.

"And what would I be doing during the day when y'all are out there in the sand having fun?" Celia asked.

"There is always shade made by the house, at different angles during the day, depending on the movement of the sun," Tommy explained.

Mandie realized everyone was finished with the meal and Mrs. Patton has risen. "Coffee in the drawing room," she was saying to the maid.

Everyone else stood up, and Mrs. Patton led the way into the drawing room.

Mandie reluctantly went with the group. She wanted to get away and slip upstairs. Then, as she was walking along with her friends down the hallway, she suddenly remembered her cat. "Oh, Tommy, Snowball is in my room, and he needs something to eat."

All the young people stopped.

"I would imagine that one of the maids has seen to that," Tommy said.

"I think I'd better go see," Mandie replied. Before anyone could object she started in the other direction down the hall and called back, "I'll only be a few minutes."

"Please hurry," Tommy said.

Mandie ran up the huge staircase and down the long hallway to the room she and Celia were occupying. Pushing open the door, she looked around for her white cat. He was not in the room.

Just as Mandie was leaving the room, she ran into Cheechee, the young maid.

"Dat white cat be in de kitchen eatin' his supper," the girl said and then turned and ran down the hallway.

"Thank you," Mandie called after her, but the maid didn't look back.

"Well," Mandie said to herself and started down the hallway in the opposite direction to return downstairs and join the others. She wondered why the young girl seemed to be afraid of her.

When she joined her friends in the drawing room, she said to them, "Cheechee ran away from me like she was terrified of something."

Tommy laughed and said, "Don't you remember? When y'all came to visit us at the beach house it was Cheechee who was trying to scare you."

"I remember that but I'd think she would have forgotten about that by now," Mandie replied as she sat down on the settee next to Celia.

When Joe looked at her, Mandie added, "It was something silly that Josephine had put her up to. Anyhow, she said Snowball is in the kitchen eating his supper, so I suppose he's all right."

Tizzy came in with a cart holding the coffee and dessert. As she went past the settee where the group of young people were sitting, Mandie asked, "Do you know if my cat is eating in the kitchen?"

"He sho' is, eatin' ev'rything in sight. He gwine be a fat cat one of dese days," Tizzy replied as she went on toward Mrs. Patton.

Mandie smiled and said to her friends, "Every place I take Snowball to visit with me, people feed him like he had never had a bite to eat."

"That's because he is always meowing for something to eat," Jonathan said, grinning. "And he sure likes New York food."

"That's because you New York people eat so much meat," Mandie said. "At home he'll eat whatever we have, even beans and corn bread."

"But the corn bread has cracklings in it, doesn't it?" Jonathan asked. "And even I know cracklings is some kind of meat."

Tizzy came back across the room with coffee and slices of cake on a tray for the young people.

"I told you we would have coconut cake," Tommy reminded everyone.

"Oh, it's delicious," Mandie said, taking a bite of her slice.

The others agreed.

"Almost as good as chocolate cake," Joe said with a big grin.

"Maybe we'll have chocolate tomorrow," Tommy said.

While her friends were carrying on a conversion, Mandie was trying to figure out how she could get up to the third floor. At night it was probably dark up there. And she certainly didn't know her way around the third floor. Maybe she could slip off up there early tomorrow morning, that is, if she woke before Celia did.

"You must be having some serious thoughts," Joe teased her.

Mandie quickly straightened up and smiled. "Not really," she said. "It has been a long day."

"Yes, I imagine you all are tired after that long train ride," Tommy said. "If y'all would like to retire, we could always just tell my mother good-night."

"Oh no, no, Tommy, I'm not that tired," Mandie quickly told him. She looked across the room and saw her grandmother talking to Senator Morton, and Mr. Guyer was seated next to Celia's mother. She laughed and said, "I think we need to stay up and watch what goes on with our elders."

Her friends looked at the others and laughed.

"Somehow or other I'll catch up with Grandmother and get a chance to talk," Mandie sighed.

"All we need to do is get her away from Senator Morton so she wouldn't have anyone to talk to," Joe teased.

"Oh, but then she would probably be talking to my father," Jonathan reminded him.

"Do you think they are really friends now after having not spoken for all those years?" Celia asked.

"My grandmother and Jonathan's father? Maybe. Grandmother does not always act out what she is actually thinking," Mandie said.

"Neither does my father," Jonathan said. "His actions can be very deceiving sometimes."

Mandie looked across the room and noticed that all the adults seemed to be rising.

Then her mother spoke to her. "Amanda, we are all going outside for a walk, if you young people care to join us."

Mandie quickly looked at her friends and asked, "Do y'all want to go walk?"

"Not really, but I suppose we should," Joe said, rising from his chair.

"I need some exercise," Celia agreed as she, too, stood up.

"Guess we might as well all go," Jonathan added.

The young people followed the adults out the front door, but when the adults turned to the left to walk in that direction, Tommy quickly said, "Why don't we walk this way? They are heading for the water. This way goes toward the city." He turned right and the group followed.

Tommy gave a description of the people who

lived in the mansions they passed, some of it good and some of it bad.

"Now, the people in this house, the Yertzens, are newcomers, and they are not very friendly with the local people. It seems they came here from out West somewhere and are very wealthy, but no one knows where they got it," Tommy was saying as they slowed down past a huge two-story mansion.

"They must have lived in New York at some time or other, because that's the way New Yorkers live," Jonathan said as they walked on.

"And the family who lives here," Tommy said of the next house, which was quite a distance from the other one, "these people are a local family from way back, and everyone knows where they got their money."

"They do?" Mandie asked.

Tommy looked down at her and said, "Sure. All the families with inherited wealth like to brag about it. Therefore, everyone knows they are honest because they inherited their money. They didn't make it with dishonest businesses."

"Do you mean some of these people with lots of money didn't make it honestly?" Celia asked.

"Let's say a little dishonesty," Tommy replied. "They didn't go by social standards to make their wealth."

"My goodness, I didn't know you had such people living here in Charleston," Mandie said in surprise.

"Oh, Mandie, there are honest and dishonest people in every city. It just happens that the old-timers are nosy and learn all these things about any newcomers who move here," Tommy explained with a laugh.

Mandie looked up at Joe and asked, "I don't know of any dishonest people living in Franklin, North Carolina, do you, Joe?"

"No, but I imagine everyone there has lived there forever," Joe replied. "And Franklin is not a large city like Charleston here."

"Now, this house here," Tommy continued, "the people who own it are not living in it at the present but have leased it out to some strangers who will have nothing to do with anyone else. Therefore, no one knows anything about them, except my sister, Josephine."

"Josephine?" Celia asked.

"Yes, for some reason or other she has become friends with them, and my mother does not like that one bit. They have a daughter about her age, and she slips off now and then and comes down here," Tommy continued.

"How do you know she does that if you all are not friendly with these people?" Jonathan asked.

"My mother has Tizzy spying on Josephine sometimes in order to keep up with her, and Tizzy has seen her go in this house," Tommy explained. "But of course when my mother asks Josephine about it she just says she was walking past the house when the girl living there came out and talked to her. However, my mother does know that Josephine goes into the house and plans to catch her one of these days."

"From what you've been telling us I'd hate to be in Josephine's shoes," Robert said.

"Rest assured my mother will put a stop to it somehow," Tommy said.

"But why can't Josephine be friends with the girl?" Mandie asked.

Tommy looked down at her and said, "Because my mother knows nothing about what kind of people they are."

Now this mystery had Mandie interested. Where she came from, people were not judged by their social status.

"Just because someone doesn't want to tell everyone all about their private affairs doesn't mean they are bad people," Mandie argued.

"Why else would they want to keep their business private?" Tommy asked.

"Where I come from people are not judged by how much wealth they have or where they got it," Joe said. "And of course since my father is the doctor in our part of North Carolina, he eventually knows everyone's business. And it doesn't matter to anyone else who is wealthy and who is not."

Jonathan grinned and spoke up. "This city sounds like a bunch of snobs." He laughed.

"I agree," Tommy replied. "But it's not me doing that. It's the old-timers who are judging the other people."

"What is this family's name where Josephine goes to visit?" Mandie asked.

"Mr. and Mrs. Warren Bedford," Tommy replied. "And the daughter is called Ernestine, and don't ask me what she looks like because I have never seen her, even though they've been living here for several years."

"You mean she never goes out?" Celia asked.

"I don't know. I've never seen her," Tommy replied.

The group had walked way past that particular house. Mandie stopped and said, "Let's walk back so I can look at that house again."

"You want to look at that house again? I can assure you, you won't see anyone there. No one ever does," Tommy replied. "All right, we should return anyway or the others will be wondering where we went at this time of the night."

He led the way back down the street. Mandie tried to see the house in the darkness, but lots of shrubbery hid most of it from view. And there was no sign of any light.

Looking up at Tommy, Mandie said, "You know what? I think we ought to find out who these people are. I could go up to the door and knock. They wouldn't know me because I don't live here."

"Oh no you don't!" Tommy quickly responded. "My mother would not like that at all and we'd be in trouble." He hurried on down the street.

Mandie caught up with him and said, "I didn't mean I'd do that tonight. Maybe tomorrow in the daylight."

"No, no, no!" Tommy adamantly told her.

"Mandie, we can't go poking into other people's business," Joe told her. "Especially when it's in another town and no connection to us."

Mandie stomped her feet and said, "All right, all right."

No one had anything else to say, and the group returned in silence to Tommy's house, where the adults were just entering the parlor.

"I think I'd like to retire now," Celia said. "It has been a long, tiresome day with all that traveling we did."

"Yes, we should all get some rest, because my mother will probably keep us going all day tomorrow doing something," Tommy agreed.

Mandie and Celia stopped by the parlor long

enough to say good-night and then went to their rooms. The boys weren't far behind them.

When Mandie opened the door to their room, she found Snowball curled up asleep in the middle of the bed.

"Thank goodness he is here and I don't have to go get him," Mandie said as she began to get ready for bed.

"And thank goodness we can finally relax," Celia said, yawning. "I am awfully tired." She turned to look at Mandie. "We forgot to ask what time we're supposed to get up for breakfast."

"Maybe we'll just sleep right through it," Mandie said, laughing. "However, I imagine someone will come to wake us." As she changed into her night-clothes, she said, "This town is full of strange people, isn't it?"

"I was thinking the same thing, but I didn't want to say that because, after all, this is Tommy's home," Celia said, brushing out her long hair.

"In a way I wish Josephine would come home, because she gets involved in everything and we might find out things from her," Mandie said, reaching to pull down the counterpane on the bed and displacing Snowball, who protested.

"Maybe Josephine will come home while we are here," Celia said. "Tommy doesn't know when she's due back."

Mandie lay awake a long time, even though she was tired. She would like to sneak up to the third floor, but not in the dark in the middle of the night. Maybe she would wake up early enough before breakfast.

Then, too, she kept wondering about those people named Bedford. They were probably just common people and didn't want to mix with the wealthy crowd that Tommy's family belonged to. And she decided that wealthy circles must be a bunch of snobs. And she didn't think she would want to live in Charleston among such people.

Right now she was tired. Maybe tomorrow things would look better.

Chapter 5 / A Discovery

Mandie was angry with herself the next morning. She overslept and would not have time to go up to the third floor. When she opened her eyes Celia was sliding out of bed to get dressed. And at the same time the door to the hall opened.

"Breakfast in fifteen minutes," Cheechee announced as she stuck her head in the doorway.

"Fifteen minutes?" Mandie exclaimed, jumping out of bed.

"Dat's right," the young maid said and closed the door as she stepped back into the hallway.

Mandie hurried to the wardrobe to find something to put on as Celia pulled down a dress.

"Oh, I should have already been up," Mandie mumbled to herself as she found a blue cotton dress and snatched it from the hanger.

"Yes, me too," Celia said, quickly pulling on her dress.

"They sure don't give us much time to dress," Mandie continued mumbling as she shed her night-clothes and put on the blue dress.

"Maybe Cheechee forgot to let us know in time," Celia said, buttoning the bodice of her dress.

"She probably put us off till last because I believe she is still afraid of me," Mandie said, hurrying to the bureau to brush her hair. "She probably thinks I'm angry with her for that trick she played on me when I was here before."

"I wonder if the boys have already gone downstairs," Celia said, tying back her hair with a ribbon.

"Come on. We'll find out," Mandie said, leading the way to the door. She glanced back at Snowball, who was still sitting on the bed. "I'll have to remember to ask for some breakfast for Snowball." She opened the door and went out into the hallway.

Celia followed as Mandie stepped across the hall and knocked on the door to the room Joe was sharing with Jonathan. There was no answer.

Going to the door to the next room, Celia knocked on it and did not receive any response. "I suppose Robert and Tommy have already gone down, too."

"Well, we sure are the cow's tail," Mandie muttered. "Come on, let's go." She hurried toward the staircase.

When they got down to the main hallway, they met up with Tizzy.

"Ev'rybody dun in de breakfast room," she told the girls. She pointed as she said, "Dat way."

"Thank you, Tizzy," Mandie replied as she and Celia continued on their way.

The girls caught up with Joe, Tommy, Robert, and Jonathan just as they were entering the breakfast room.

"Well, y'all finally got here," Joe teased.

"We thought perhaps you weren't coming down today," Jonathan added.

"Y'all almost didn't make it yourselves," Mandie replied with a big smile.

"We were right behind y'all," Celia said as she stopped next to Robert.

As the group entered the breakfast room, Mandie quickly looked to see if her grandmother was there. She was seated beside Jane Hamilton on the other side of the table and they were both eating. The other adults were helping their plates at the long buffet of food.

"My grandmother and your mother must have been the first ones here," Mandie told Celia.

"Yes, they must have been hungry," Celia agreed with a big smile.

"What are we doing today?" Joe asked Tommy as they stood in line.

Mandie quickly turned to listen.

"I believe my mother decided you all should just have a day of rest before we do anything else," Tommy replied.

"You mean we can just eat and sleep today?" Jonathan asked, grinning.

"Whatever you wish," Tommy replied, laughing at Jonathan's remark.

"So we can do just anything we want to, then?" Mandie asked.

"Yes," Tommy told her.

"Like inspect the third floor and walk by that house again where the Bedfords live?" Mandie asked as the group moved closer to the buffet.

Tommy looked at her, smiled, and said, "Well, depends on how you want to go about that."

Celia and Robert moved up to the buffet and Mandie quickly followed them. The adults had filled their plates and were taking places at the table. She picked up a plate and began putting food on it as she talked.

"We just go up to the third floor, look around, and listen for any noise there may be up there," Mandie said, frowning as she almost dropped the bacon she was placing on her plate. "And we could take a walk down the street like we did last night and go past the Bedfords' house."

"That sounds all right if you don't plan on stopping at the Bedfords' house," Tommy replied. "However, I would never agree to stopping in front of their house, especially not in the daytime when they could see us. That is definite because my mother would be really angry if we did."

Mandie quickly filled her plate and turned to find a place at the table. She noticed that Senator Morton had sat down beside her grandmother and Mr. Guyer had taken the seat next to Mrs. Hamilton. The other adults were at the far end of the table.

"Let's sit here," Mandie told her friends as she set her plate down at the end away from the adults. The others followed.

Tizzy quickly came to fill their cups with coffee. And Mandie remembered Snowball. "Tizzy, I left my cat in my room," she said, "Would you please see that he gets something to eat?"

"I sho' will, missy," Tizzy said, smiling at her as she poured the hot, rich coffee into her coffee cup. "Don't you worry none 'bout dat cat. I take care o' him."

"Thank you," Mandie replied.

The young people talked about various topics as they ate. Mandie kept watching her grandmother now and then to see what she was doing. Then she saw Mrs. Taft and Mrs. Hamilton leave the table after finishing their meal, and Senator Morton and Mr. Guyer followed them out of the room.

"I wish somebody would get Senator Morton away from my grandmother for a little while so I could talk to her," Mandie said, blowing out her breath.

Her friends turned to watch the four adults leave the room.

"We'll have to think up some way to do that," Jonathan said.

"I think that would be hard to do," Joe said.

"Mandie, maybe I could ask my mother to help somehow," Celia suggested.

"What if I ask Senator Morton to tell us about the latest doings in Washington? Do you think he would?" Tommy asked.

"He might agree to that, but Mandie's grandmother might want to listen, also," Robert said.

"Probably, because my grandfather was also a senator and I suppose my grandmother is still interested in politics," Mandie told them.

"Mandie, I would just walk right up to her and say, 'Grandmother, may I have a private word with you?' Don't you think that would work?" Joe suggested.

"You don't think I would be rude to say that in front of Senator Morton?" Mandie questioned.

"No," her friends chorused.

The other adults, Elizabeth and John Shaw and Mr. and Mrs. Patton, rose from the table and walked by the young people on their way out the door.

"Amanda, today is a free day to do whatever you please, rest or whatever, but please don't get into any trouble," Elizabeth Shaw told Mandie as she stopped by their end of the table.

"Yes, ma'am," Mandie replied. "I won't." Her mother and the others left the room. She looked at her friends. Everyone had finished their breakfast. "If everyone's finished, let's go."

"Third floor?" Tommy questioned her as everyone rose from the table.

"Yes," Mandie said with a big smile.

As they followed Tommy out of the room, Mandie said, "Let's look in the parlor and see if my grandmother is in there before we go upstairs."

"If she is I don't imagine she is alone," Celia remarked as they started down the hallway.

Celia was right. Mrs. Taft was sitting in the parlor, but so were all the other adults.

"Oh well," Mandie said. "Let's go upstairs."

"Come on, this way. We'll go up the back stairs," Tommy told them, leading the way to the rear hallway.

Sliding double doors closed off the end of the hallway. Tommy pushed them open, revealing an ornately paneled corridor at the center and a winding carved staircase going up.

"This is the servants' stairway," Tommy explained as he led the way up the steps.

"Won't they resent our intrusion into their territory?" Jonathan asked.

"I don't think so," Tommy said. "Not at this time of day, anyway. They are all probably in different parts of the house working right now."

"What would they say if we met up with any of them back here?" Mandie asked, closely following Tommy.

"More than likely nothing," Tommy replied. He came to the landing for the second floor. Looking back at his guests, he added, "One more flight," and continued up.

From there up all the shutters were closed on the windows along the stairs, making it dark inside. However, Tommy knew where all the electric switches were and he kept turning them on as they went.

"I'm glad you have electricity in this house," Mandie commented. "Otherwise we would have to carry lamps all the way up."

"So am I," Tommy looked back to say. "But my mother and father were some of the first in Charleston to hook on to the electricity when it became available."

"We got it at our school in Asheville, you know, before your school got it," Celia said. "All those funny-looking wires hanging down from the ceiling with a light bulb on the end."

"We still don't have electricity at Mr. Chadwick's School," Robert said. "He has said he saw no reason to rush into anything that new."

"Here we are," Tommy said, pushing open a door at the top of the stairs. He reached inside, found a switch, and turned on the electric lights.

Mandie looked around the third-floor hallway as they entered it.

The group stopped behind her.

"It looks almost like the hallway on the second floor, doesn't it?" Mandie said, gazing down the length of it where small tables, chairs, and settees were placed.

"Yes, if you walked in your sleep and woke up up here you'd probably think you were on the second floor," Joe teased.

"Now, Mandie, you've been up on the widow's

walk, remember?" Tommy said, stepping over to a small door and opening it, revealing a spiral staircase inside. "You see? This is the entrance. Remember?"

"Oh yes, I remember very well," Mandie replied with a smile. "I thought I'd never get up to it that time with you." She turned away from the entrance to the widow's walk. "But whereabouts did the servants hear that noise?" She looked down the hallway.

"Oh, it was up near the front of the house," Tommy said, closing the door to the spiral staircase. "Come on, I'll show you."

Tommy walked across the back hallway and opened a door going into the main third-floor corridor. "This way," he told the others.

Mandie and her friends followed Tommy down a long hallway to the intersection of a cross hall. Here, Tommy turned left. All the doors to the many rooms they passed were closed. This reminded Mandie of the confusing network of corridors in Jonathan Guyer's home in New York.

Mandie glanced back at Jonathan behind her and said, "They keep all their doors closed like y'all do in your house."

"Doesn't everybody keep doors closed to rooms they are not using?" Jonathan asked.

"We don't at my house," Mandie said. "My mother says all the doors should be left open just a tiny bit so the rooms won't smell stale."

Tommy stopped and looked at her. "So you think our rooms must smell stale?" he asked, grinning at her. Then he stepped over to a closed door and opened it, revealing a large bedroom. "Smell."

"Oh, Tommy, I didn't mean that," Mandie said,

looking beyond him into the room. Her friends also stopped to look.

"My mother keeps the doors slightly open all the time in our house, too," Celia added.

"Well, we don't have a large house, so all the doors are open or closed according to what is going on, I suppose," Joe said.

"I had not even thought about that, but I don't remember whether our doors stay open or closed," Robert said. "I promise to let you know when I go home and look." He smiled at Celia.

"I suppose the noise your servants heard up here was in a room with the door closed," Mandie told Tommy.

He closed the door to the room he had opened and continued on down the hallway. "Yes, since we close the doors to all the rooms," he replied, grinning down at Mandie. "This way."

Tommy stopped at the far end of the corridor and opened a door. "The noise seemed to be coming from inside this room, Rouster said, but of course the servants didn't wait to investigate—they fled in fright," he explained. He stood back so the others could look inside.

Mandie walked on into the room. It was a nicely furnished bedroom, and she went over to look out the window, which she noticed was not shuttered.

"This is over the side of the front of the house, isn't it?" she asked Tommy as the others followed her.

"Yes. In fact, this room is connected with the outside staircase," Tommy said. He went over to what Mandie had thought was a door to an adjoining room and opened it, revealing steps going down outside.

Mandie frowned as she thought about the doors.

"You close all the doors but you don't bother to lock the door to the outside like this one," she said, looking at Tommy.

"Yes, I suppose you are right. No one has ever thought about locking this door," he replied.

"Someone could come up those stairs and get into the house," Celia remarked.

"But why would anyone want to come up such steep narrow steps to get inside the house?" Tommy asked.

"For no good reason," Jonathan said. "At least in New York we do keep all the outside doors locked."

Mandie walked around the room, looking at the spotless furniture. Then she stopped, gazed up at Tommy, and asked, "What did the noise sound like?"

"What do you mean, what did it sound like? It was a noise, that's all Rouster said," Tommy replied.

"What I mean is, was it a metal-like sound or a paper-rattling sound or a glass sound or what?" Mandie asked.

"I have no idea," Tommy said. "Rouster just said the servants heard a noise somewhere around this area of the house."

"Oh, shucks!" Mandie exclaimed as she stomped her foot. "Tommy Patton, you would never make a detective!"

"Why, I had just recently decided that when I finish school I might set up a private detective agency," Tommy teased. "I suppose I'd have to get you to come and run it for me."

"No, thank you, if I am going to run such a business it will be my own," Mandie replied, also grinning.

"Mandie, please don't go getting ideas of becoming a detective when you finish school," Celia said. "It would be an unsafe job for a woman."

"Unsafe?" Jonathan spoke up. "She is already running into all these unsafe mysteries everywhere she goes."

"She will outgrow that idea," Joe said, grinning at her.

Mandie ignored the conversation, walked over to the huge bureau, and opened the top drawer. She looked inside, surprised at what it held. "Tommy, this drawer is full of books," she said.

Tommy and the others came to look. He shuffled through the books and said, "These are all very old books. I have no idea as to what they are doing in a bureau drawer." He looked puzzled.

"That sure is a strange place to store books," Joe remarked.

Tommy began opening the other drawers. They were all empty.

"Have you ever seen these books before in another place, like on a bookshelf?" Jonathan asked.

"I'm not sure," Tommy said. "We have quite a few books in different shelves and cabinets throughout the house. I suppose these must belong to us. But why would they be in one of our bureaus like this?"

"Maybe all the bookshelves are full everywhere and there was no other place to put them," Celia suggested.

Mandie suddenly had an idea. "Maybe there are things stored in other rooms in bureaus and things," she said.

Tommy straightened up to look at her and said,

"Now, that kind of investigation would take time to accomplish."

"Not if we scattered out and each one of us searched so many rooms each," Mandie said with a big grin.

"Mandie, please don't go getting that kind of idea," Joe moaned. "That sounds like work to me."

"Yes, it does," Jonathan agreed. "Besides, I thought we were going to walk past that house where the people called Bedford live."

"But we have the whole day free," Mandie replied. "We could do this up here, and after the noontime meal we could go walking."

"No, no, no, not unless you want to bake in the afternoon sun," Tommy protested. "The weather is hot in the afternoon, too hot to go strolling around town."

"Well, then," Mandie said thoughtfully, "why don't we go for the walk now and then this afternoon we come back up here and search." She looked up at Tommy.

"Well, I suppose we could do that," Tommy reluctantly agreed and then asked, "but what are we looking for in the other bureau drawers and things?"

"More books," Mandie replied and then added, "or whatever."

"Come on," Tommy said. "Let's go for a stroll and we can discuss this while we walk."

"We need to get our hats, Mandie," Celia reminded her. "I freckle in the sunshine."

"All right," Mandie agreed. "We'll get them. Tommy, will you please explain how we can get our room without going through all those hallways again?"

"That's easy. Your room is almost directly

beneath this one," Tommy explained. "I'll show you and then I'll wait in the front hall for y'all."

The boys went on with Tommy after he showed the girls their room.

Mandie opened the door and found Snowball curled up asleep on the bed. "Oh, I need to take Snowball out for some air," she said, quickly picking up his red leash from the bureau and fastening it to his collar as he stood and stretched.

"I'll help you with him," Celia said, quickly putting on her straw hat.

Mandie found her hat and stood before the mirror to fasten it on with a large hatpin. "Celia, do you think we might see that Bedford girl when we walk past that house?" she asked.

"I don't know, Mandie," Celia replied, straightening her hat before the mirror. "Anyhow, please remember that Tommy said we could not stop or speak to anyone there."

"Yes, I know," Mandie said, opening the door as she led Snowball out into the hall on his leash. "But what are we supposed to do if that girl sees us and speaks?"

Celia frowned and said, "I still wouldn't speak to her."

They hurried down the hallway to the main staircase.

"Well, at least we can look at her if she appears," Mandie said. And she would really like to know what the girl looked like, since she had become friends with Josephine. She didn't see how anyone could be Josephine's friend because of the girl's attitude and manners. She was Tommy's sister, but she was adopted, so maybe that made the difference.

They hurried on to meet the boys in the front hallway.

Chapter 6 / The Girl

Mandie and her friends walked toward the section of huge mansions where the Bedfords lived. The sunshine was already becoming hot and there were few people on the streets. But Mandie was not conscious of the heat. She was hoping the Bedford girl would be outside her house and she could get a good look at her.

"Snowball, slow down," Mandie told the white cat as she tightened her grip on the red leash when he tried to run ahead.

Snowball looked back at her and growled.

"What did Snowball say?" Tommy teased as he walked along beside Mandie.

Mandie grinned up at him and said, "I believe he said, 'I won't do it.' "

Joe, walking on the other side of Mandie, said, "He is a very independent cat. And you should see him chase dogs."

Jonathan stepped forward from behind and said, "Isn't that the Bedfords' house on the next block? The one with all those bushes in the yard?"

"Yes, it is," Tommy replied.

Mandie was overwhelmed with the many, many

huge mansions in Charleston. "Why does everyone in this town build such huge houses?" she asked as they walked on.

"Some areas have huge houses like these, but other parts of town have much smaller, cheaper houses, even shacks now and then," Tommy explained. "And not all the people living in these big houses are wealthy. Some of them are living more or less on the credit."

"On the credit?" Mandie questioned. "Why would anyone want to live in such a house they can't really afford?"

"It probably makes them feel rich," Tommy said with a big grin.

They crossed a side street, and the Bedford house was in that block.

"Let's don't walk too fast so I can look at the house," Mandie said to her friends as she slowed down.

It was built of stone and rose three stories in the air, but there were very few windows in it. A flower-covered wall closed off any view of the front door and porch. As they came to the lacy black iron gate, Mandie tried to see through tiny open places in the pattern, but she remembered that Tommy had said very emphatically that they were not to stop in front of the house.

"Keep walking," Tommy reminded her in a loud whisper as he came up behind her, and the others moved on.

Mandie reluctantly followed her friends. She looked up at Tommy and said, "You said we couldn't stop in front of the house. However, you didn't say how many times we could walk past it." She smiled at him.

"Twice," Tommy replied. "We just passed it and we will pass it again on our way back. Twice."

The young people walked one more block, which was a long one, and then turned around to go back toward Tommy's house. Mandie slowed down and let them all get ahead of her so she could have a clear view of the Bedford house when she passed it. Snowball pulled at the leash and tried to walk faster.

Joe dropped back to walk beside Mandie. "I suppose we'll have the noon meal before we begin that search on the third floor, don't you think?" he asked.

"Yes, I would imagine so," Mandie agreed. She looked ahead as they approached the front of the Bedford house again.

Tommy, Celia, Jonathan, and Robert all paused to look back. And at that moment Snowball gave a strong jerk to his leash and it snapped open, giving him freedom to run.

Mandie, holding the leash in her hand, started after the white cat. "Snowball, come back here," she yelled at him.

Snowball leaped into the air and landed on top of the rock wall in front of the Bedfords' house. He paused to look back at his mistress and then dived off the other side into the yard.

Mandie ran to the gate to peep through, trying to see where he had gone. "Snowball, come here!" she called to him but couldn't see him.

All her friends had rushed to her side and were trying to look into the yard.

Mandie pushed at the gate, but it wouldn't budge. She raised her foot to kick it and it still wouldn't move. "Snowball!" she kept yelling.

Joe joined in. "Snowball, you cat, get back

here," he called, also trying to see inside the yard.

Then the whole group added their calls.

Mandie looked at the high wall and the locked gate, raised her long skirts, and tried to climb the gate. Tommy rushed up behind and pulled her down. "Mandie! You can't do that!" he told her.

Before Mandie could reply as she straightened her clothes, she saw a girl behind the shrubbery bushes inside the yard, and the girl was holding Snowball.

"Give me my cat!" she yelled at the girl.

"He's mine now. He came into my yard," the girl yelled back, staying behind the bushes.

Tommy moved closer to Mandie and called to the girl, "Bring us that cat. He doesn't belong to you."

"Let's all go over the wall and get him," Jonathan told the others as he prepared to climb up the post and get on top of the wall.

"No, no, Jonathan," Tommy said, coming to Jonathan's side.

"Why not? That's the only way we're going to get that cat back," Jonathan replied, still standing by the post.

"Let's stand still here and think this situation out," Tommy told the group.

"There's nothing to think out," Jonathan said.

"Well, while we are standing here thinking, that girl has disappeared with Snowball," Mandie protested.

Joe looked down at Mandie and asked, "Do you want me to go over the wall and get him? It wouldn't be any problem for me to cross that wall."

"Yes, yes, please, Joe, go get Snowball," Mandie

immediately replied, tears brimming in her blue eyes.

"And I will go with you," Jonathan added.

Tommy stepped forward and confronted Joe and Jonathan. "You all will be causing a lot of trouble if you trespass into that yard," he told them.

"I'll worry about the consequences. In the meantime, I intend going after that cat," Joe said, turning to look up at the wall.

"And I'm with you," Jonathan added.

Celia and Robert stood by watching and did not participate in the conversation. Tommy silently stepped back beside them.

"I go first," Joe told Jonathan as he pulled himself up the post and managed to get on top of the wall.

"I'm right behind you," Jonathan said. He quickly joined Joe on the wall. They looked down into the yard.

Mandie watched and asked, "Can you see Snowball? Has that girl still got him?" She tried to peek through the openwork of the gate.

"I don't see him or the girl, but I'm going to jump down inside," Joe said, giving a leap down into the yard.

Jonathan quickly followed.

Mandie waited but there was nothing but silence in the yard. She listened but couldn't hear Joe or Jonathan moving about behind the wall. And there was no sound of Snowball. She figured the boys might be trying to slip up on the girl and catch her unawares and then grab Snowball. So she didn't call to them.

Celia stepped up to Mandie and reached for her hand. "I hope they get Snowball," she whispered.

"Thank you," Mandie whispered back, squeezing Celia's hand.

Mandie looked back and saw that Tommy and Robert had moved away a few feet and were talking in low tones. She knew Tommy was upset with what they were doing and that he would probably be in trouble with his mother about it. But Snowball had caused all this, and Mandie thought to herself that she should have left him at home in North Carolina. If she ever came to visit the Pattons again, Snowball would definitely stay at home.

Suddenly Joe appeared on the other side of the iron gate. And he was whispering, "He's not here. She must have taken him into the house."

"Knock on the door, and whoever answers it, tell them to give you my cat," Mandie replied in a whisper.

"All right," Joe agreed and quickly vanished among the thick bushes in the yard.

Mandie stood there, practically holding her breath. She heard the knock on the door and then in a few moments there were voices, but she could not hear them well enough to know what was being said. And then there was complete silence.

She turned to Celia, who was standing by her, and whispered, "Can you hear anything? What happened to everyone in there?"

"I believe someone did come to the door when Joe knocked," Celia said.

"Yes, but what happened? I don't hear a thing now," Mandie said. "Do you think it could have been that Bedford girl?"

"It could have been," Celia agreed. "But Joe must have gone inside the house, because the voices stopped."

"Jonathan seems to have completely disappeared," Mandie said to Celia as they both tried to see through the gate.

Suddenly Jonathan popped up in front of them on the other side of the gate. "Shh! Joe went inside the house," he whispered.

"Why didn't you go with him?" Mandie asked.

"We decided not to let them know there are two of us, so one of us can stay outside and watch," Jonathan explained.

"Who came to the door? Was it the girl?" Mandie asked.

"No, it was a man, a real old man," Jonathan explained. "The girl must have gone inside the house with Snowball before we jumped the wall. We haven't seen her at all."

"Can you see the door from here if Joe comes back out?" Mandie asked.

"Not too clearly. There are so many bushes in this yard," Jonathan replied.

"I wonder why Joe went inside that house anyway. Why didn't he just tell the man we wanted my cat?" Mandie said.

"I don't know. As far as I could hear, the man just opened the door and started saying, 'Come in the house, come in the house,' and didn't give Joe a chance to say anything," Jonathan whispered through the gate. Then he asked, "What are Tommy and Robert doing? I can't see them from here."

Mandie glanced back at the two boys, who were still standing at the edge of the road talking. "Still talking," she told Jonathan.

All of a sudden Joe came up behind Jonathan with Snowball in his arms. "Now we have to figure out how to get back over that wall with this cat," he told Jonathan.

"Oh, you got him, Joe! Thank you, thank you," Mandie cried excitedly as she got a glimpse of white fur through an opening in the gate.

"Why didn't they unlock the gate to let you out?" Jonathan asked.

"The old man was not very bright," Joe replied. "I couldn't make him understand very much. We were standing in the parlor and Snowball came running into the room. I snatched him up and headed for the front door."

"Did you see that Bedford girl?" Mandie asked.

"Yes, I only got a glimpse of her and also another girl in a room down the hallway. Soon as they saw me they disappeared," Joe replied. "Now, let's get this cat across the wall, Jonathan."

"I'll climb up on top of the wall and you hand him up to me," Jonathan said. "And then I'll just drop him down the other side and Mandie can catch him." He quickly made his way to the top of the wall.

Mandie stepped back to watch.

"Here he is," Joe called from the other side as he tossed Snowball up to Jonathan.

Snowball growled and huffed up his fur as he landed on the wall. And before Jonathan could catch him he jumped down and landed at Mandie's feet. She quickly snatched him up.

"Oh, Snowball, you are such a troublemaker," Mandie told him as she held him tightly in her arms.

Jonathan jumped down and Joe followed.

Tommy and Robert walked over to them. "I'm glad you were able to get Snowball," Tommy said to

Joe and Jonathan. "I think we'd better get on back to the house."

Joe stepped in front of Tommy and said, "Hold on a minute. I saw the girl who was in the yard. She was in another room in the house with another girl." He paused and looked directly at Tommy. "And that other girl looked very much like your sister, Josephine."

"What!" Tommy exclaimed as the others gathered around in excitement. He took a deep breath and said, "I'm sure you are mistaken. Josephine is at the beach with friends. Now, let's get back." He started walking toward his house.

"I think you should ask your mother to check on Josephine," Joe insisted as he kept up with Tommy.

Mandie thought about things for a moment and then said, "Maybe this Bedford girl was visiting at the same place as Josephine was and they came back to the Bedfords' house together."

"I don't think so," Tommy insisted as he hurried on.

"Tommy, I'm sorry Snowball caused so much trouble. I'll see that he doesn't get outside again unless I am holding him and he can't get away," Mandie said, trying to keep up with the boys, who seemed to be in such a hurry.

Tommy didn't answer.

"I'll help you with him, Mandie," Celia told her.

"He's no trouble. That was a lot of fun," Jonathan said, grinning at the girls.

"Fun? Oh, Jonathan, I was worried sick about him," Mandie said, holding the cat tightly in her arms.

Jonathan stepped up close to Mandie and Celia

and whispered, "Just think. Snowball was the cause of us finding out a secret."

Mandie looked at him and repeated, "A secret?"

"Yes, that Josephine is not where she's supposed to be. I imagine some fur will fly about that," Jonathan continued whispering.

"But it might not have been her," Celia said.

"What do you think Mrs. Patton will do if someone tells her that Josephine is probably at the Bedfords' house?" Mandie asked as she watched the boys moving on ahead of them.

"First of all, someone will have to prove that was Josephine in that house," Jonathan said.

"And how are they going to do that?" Celia asked.

"Well, now, if they would like, I'll be glad to go back and knock on that front door and inquire," Jonathan said with a big grin.

"That's no sign you will be able to get inside the house," Mandie reminded him.

"I can guarantee you if I knock on that door and someone opens it I will get inside that house," Jonathan said.

Joe came up to Mandie as they walked. "What are you going to do with Snowball for the rest of our visit?" he asked.

"I'll keep him shut up in our room," Mandie said, glancing at the red leash in her hand. "And I'll need to be sure the catch on this leash is working."

Joe reached for the leash, looked at it, and said, "I'll fix it for you. The little hook that clasps onto his collar is bent. It'll be all right."

They finally came to the front of the Pattons' house. Mandie took a deep breath and braced herself to face the storm that Tommy seemed to expect from his mother when she was told they had been at the Bedfords' house.

All the young people fell silent as Tommy led the way and held the front door open for everyone. "I believe everyone is already in the parlor waiting for us to return for the noon meal," he said, waving them on toward the parlor.

Mandie stopped in the hallway and said, "Tommy, I need to go up to my room and leave Snowball. I'll be right back."

"I'll go with you," Celia quickly told her, and the two girls hurried down the wide hallway toward the main staircase.

"If you could loan me a hammer and screwdriver, Tommy, I could repair this leash in half a minute," Joe said.

"All right, come on back to the workroom," Tommy said, and the boys followed him toward the back.

In Mandie and Celia's room the girls quickly freshened up while Snowball curled up on the bed to take a nap.

"I dread facing my mother when she finds out what we've been doing," Mandie said, brushing her long blond hair.

"It was an accident that Snowball got loose, so I don't think anyone can blame you too much," Celia said, retying the sash on her pale green dress.

Mandie grinned at Celia and said, "I just hope that *is* Josephine at the Bedfords' house. That will take part of the trouble off me, because if it is, we did find her and Mrs. Patton ought to appreciate that."

"Yes, Mrs. Patton will probably be more upset

about that than what happened to Snowball," Celia agreed.

"I'm just sorry that Tommy seemed to get upset with us. I don't know what else we could have done. We had to get Snowball back," Mandie said.

"And our mothers, Mandie," Celia reminded her. "What do you think they will do when they hear our story?"

Mandie thought for a moment and said, "I'm not sure what my mother will do, but I'm hoping my grandmother will be around to take my side of it."

"I do, too," Celia agreed.

"In fact, maybe I will have a chance to talk with my grandmother about that letter I received from Lily," Mandie said.

"If your grandmother is not too engrossed in conversation with Senator Morton or Mr. Guyer." She grinned at Mandie.

"We might as well go find out," Mandie said, laying down her hairbrush and going to the door. "And I want to be sure Snowball is shut up in here." She allowed Celia to step out into the hallway and then firmly closed the door and checked it to be sure it was closed.

When they came to the door of the parlor, Mandie instantly spotted her grandmother sitting alone on the far side of the room. The senator and Mr. Guyer were not in the room. She quickly walked over to Mrs. Taft.

"Grandmother, I need to talk to you about something," Mandie said, sitting down on the stool by Mrs. Taft. Celia went to the other side of the room where her mother, Mandie's mother, Uncle John Shaw, and Mrs. Patton were all talking.

"What is it, dear?" Mrs. Taft asked, smiling at Mandie.

"Guess what? I received a letter from Lily Masterson. Remember her on the ship when we went to Europe?" Mandie asked, trying to hurry.

"Of course, I certainly do remember that girl and her little sister. And I have wondered whatever became of them," Mrs. Taft replied.

"They are back home in Fountain Inn, South Carolina," Mandie explained. "And Lily wrote in her letter that if we are ever that way we should come visit." Mandie paused to look up at her grandmother. "Do you think we could really go visit them, Grandmother? Do you think it's possible?"

"Yes, I believe it would be possible to go visit them some day," Mrs. Taft replied with a smile.

"But, Grandmother, I thought maybe we could stop there on our way back home if the train goes through there," Mandie excitedly suggested.

"We'll see, dear, we'll see. Now here comes Senator Morton," Mrs. Taft said, looking across the room.

Mandie took a deep breath and stood up to join Celia. At least her grandmother was now aware of the letter and would have time to think about it while they were here at the Pattons' house. Maybe she would be able to figure how they could go visit.

Chapter 7 / Where Did That Come From?

When everyone went in to the noon meal, the young people were grouped together near the end of the long table. They could carry on their own conversations without being heard by the adults at the head of the table. On the other hand, Mandie could not listen to what her grandmother and the others were talking about.

Her friends were mostly silent at the table, and she felt it was because of the escapade with Snowball. Sitting directly across from Tommy, she asked him, "Aren't you going to tell your mother about that other girl in the Bedfords' house?"

"I haven't decided yet," Tommy replied, glancing at his mother, who seemed to be carrying on a conversation with all her guests.

"If that was Josephine I saw, I'm sure your mother would want to get her home," Joe said, sipping his coffee.

"I'm not sure I want to explain to her exactly what we were doing at the Bedfords' house," Tommy said, laying down his fork and straightening up to look across the table at Mandie.

"But you didn't do anything wrong, Tommy," Mandie said. "And I don't mind if you explain to her what happened because I don't believe I did anything wrong. I think my mother would agree with me."

"I'm sure your mother would want to know if that is your sister at the Bedfords' house so she could get her home, as Joe said," Jonathan told him.

Tommy sipped his coffee and looked at his friends. "If Josephine is out there, it's not the first time this has happened. I suppose she's all right there. It's just that my mother does not want to associate with those people because no one knows what kind of reputation they have. And also my mother wants Josephine to learn to obey. So if I tell my mother anything about what happened, she would have someone investigate and bring Josephine home if she is there." He paused, blew out his breath, and added, "And Josephine can be awfully mean sometimes. So she would probably vent her anger on all of us."

Mandie smiled at Tommy and said, "That's all right with me. I've seen her angry before when she made up all those ghost tales about this house, remember?"

"Tommy, if Josephine is all right with the Bedfords, I would leave things alone for now," Celia told him. "If we do move on to your beach house, then we should tell your mother that she may be at the Bedfords. But as long as we are here in this house and you think she is all right, then I would leave things alone."

"I've been thinking the same thing," Tommy agreed. "I'd just hate to stir up a hornet's nest and ruin y'all's vacation with us."

Mandie smiled at Tommy and said, "Then let's forget about all that for the time being and go up to the third floor and search all those drawers that we had planned on looking into."

Tommy smiled back at her and said, "That sounds like a good idea." He looked around the table at the young people and asked, "Are y'all in agreement?"

"Yes," went around the group.

As soon as the meal was finished, Tommy got them all excused from cake and coffee in the parlor and they headed for the third floor.

He led the way into the first room at the top of the stairs and told the group, "I don't know exactly what y'all are looking for, but if you find anything at all in any of the drawers, please let me know and we'll decide whether it's important or not. And let's do one room at a time."

Mandie decided just about every piece of furniture up there had some kind of drawer in it, and they all seemed to be empty.

After searching the fourth room and not finding anything at all, Joe straightened up from the drawer he had pulled out and said, "This is a hopeless cause. We should have taken time to eat some of that delicious-looking chocolate cake I saw on the sideboard."

Tommy looked at him and grinned. "I can fix that," he said. "I'll run down to the kitchen and ask Tizzy to send us some up on the dumbwaiter." He started for the door. "I'll be right back." And he went out into the hall.

Mandie glanced around the bedroom they were in and said, "Where shall we eat the cake? Let's find a table somewhere."

The group moved out into the hall and began looking in rooms for a table. Finally they opened the door to what seemed to be a very small library. One wall was lined with shelves loaded with books, and a carved mahogany library table stood in the center of the floor with chairs clustered around it.

"Oh, this is perfect," Mandie said, walking around the room. "There are six of us and there happens to be six chairs. Perfect."

"I wonder where the dumbwaiter is," Celia said. "I hope we're near it."

"Wherever it is I won't mind walking to it to pick up the cake," Joe said with a big grin.

Mandie went over to inspect the books. "A lot of these books are on the history of Charleston," she said. "This one is the British Occupation of Charleston during the Revolutionary War and here is one about Fort Sumter. And a book about the earthquake in 1886."

Joe came to look over her shoulder as she took down each book. "Charleston is full of history," he said, and looking down at Mandie, he added, "This would be a wonderful place to live when I finish my schooling."

Mandie quickly looked up at him and said, "You'd live here in Charleston? This is an awfully long way from home in North Carolina, Joe."

"Not as far as New Orleans, where I go to college," Joe said. "And you know if I am to practice law I will have to live somewhere that I can make a living."

"Oh, Joe, you could set up practice at Charley Gap or at least in Bryson City. Everyone there knows you and would give you their business I'm sure," Mandie quickly told him, frowning as she looked up into his brown eyes.

"I could, but I wouldn't make much of a living," Joe replied. "You know if my father had not inherited all his money, he would never have set up a medical practice at Charley Gap and made a living. The poor people there don't have much and want to trade chickens, corn, or whatever they have for medical help."

"Then if your father inherited a lot of money, you will inherit it from him some day since you are an only child. I'm sure Dr. Woodard would be glad to help you get started in law practice," Mandie replied, frowning as she thought about her future.

"Of course he would do anything to help me and to get me to stay close to home, but I want to do things on my own, Mandie," Joe replied. "I want to prove to myself that I can do it."

"Well, so do I," Mandie quickly told him. "I don't want all that wealth my mother and Uncle John and my grandmother have. I want to be independent."

Joe grinned at her and asked, "Independent like what?"

Mandie stuttered for a moment and then said, "Well, like having my own business. Maybe I'll set up practice as a lady detective."

"Lady detective?" Joe asked in surprise. "Mandie, you don't want to be a lady detective. Why, that could be dangerous work. You won't ever have to work. You can marry me and I'll see that you get anything you ever want."

Mandie felt her face flush, and she wouldn't look into Joe's eyes as she replied, "Joe Woodard, marriage is a long way in the future, and who knows what may transpire between now and then." She quickly turned away to look at Celia, who was opening the drawer in the table.

"I found something!" Celia exclaimed as she stood there looking into the drawer.

"What is it?" Mandie asked, quickly rushing to her side. She gasped when she saw what Celia had found.

Her friends were also curious and came to see for themselves just what was in the drawer.

"I thought maybe it was a snake," Jonathan joked.

At that moment Tommy opened the door and came into the library. "I'm glad y'all found this room," he said, walking over to a panel in the wainscoting. "I meant to tell you the dumbwaiter opens in here." He quickly slid the panel open, revealing a tray on a shelf hanging from ropes. The aroma of coffee filled the room.

"Coffee!" Jonathan said, going to inspect the contents of the tray.

"And chocolate cake," Joe added as he stepped back to look.

Tommy turned to look at the girls and Robert, who were standing in front of the library table. "Is something wrong?" he asked.

"We don't know," Mandie replied, not budging from in front of the open drawer.

"Look," Celia told Tommy, pointing to the drawer.

"What is it?" Tommy asked, coming to join them. He looked down into the drawer and picked up what Celia had found. "I can't imagine what this is doing in the library table."

"It's someone's hair," Mandie said, frowning as she stared at the piece of blond hair tied together with a blue ribbon, forming a curl.

"Yes, and I have no idea where it came from or how it got in that drawer. Was anything else in there?" Tommy asked as he bent to run his hand around the entire inside of the drawer. Not finding anything else, he straightened up and said, "Let's leave it in there until we at least eat our cake and coffee." He dropped the piece of hair back in the drawer and closed it.

Going back over to the dumbwaiter, he took a tray of coffee cups and a percolator of hot coffee from it, put them on the library table, and then took out the slices of chocolate cake.

"Ummm," said Robert. "Smells good."

"Help yourselves," Tommy told them.

Everyone settled down at the table with cake and coffee.

"Mandie, your cat was in the kitchen being well fed by Tizzy," Tommy said. "She said she would take him back up to your room when he finishes his food."

"Thanks, Tommy," Mandie said. "I meant to ask Tizzy to feed him."

"You won't have to worry about him. Tizzy will take care of him," Tommy said.

"Where is everyone? Are they all in the parlor?" Mandie asked as she sipped the hot coffee.

"I believe so. I passed the parlor door and didn't stop to look in," Tommy said. Looking around the group, he asked, "Now, what else have y'all found while I was gone?"

"Nothing," everyone chimed in.

"Do you have any idea as to whose hair that is that Celia found?" Mandie asked.

"Not offhand," Tommy replied. "My mother would probably know, but then we'd have to tell her where we found it and I imagine that is not the place where it is supposed to be. We have a whole collection of baby stuff, bibs, clothes, shoes, photos, and everything from probably a hundred years ago, but it is all supposed to be in a section of the attic that is allocated for that purpose."

"In the attic? You have an attic up above here? I thought this was absolutely the top floor," Mandie said.

"Oh no, we have a full-sized attic that goes over most of the house," Tommy explained. "The house is so tall you can't really tell it's there from the outside."

Mandie grinned at him and asked, "Are you going to show it to us?"

"I knew that question was coming," Joe teased.

"Of course," Jonathan said. "We have to see everything."

"Let's finish searching the drawers on this floor real fast and then go up there," Mandie suggested.

"I almost forgot to tell y'all," Tommy said, looking at the group. "My parents are taking all the adults out for dinner tonight, so we are on our own. Tizzy will give us supper whenever we are ready."

"So we are free without adult supervision tonight," Celia remarked, drinking her coffee and hurrying to eat her cake.

"That gives me a nice feeling, that we can do whatever we please," Jonathan said with a grin.

As everyone finished their cake and coffee and piled the dirty dishes back on the dumbwaiter, they discussed their plans for the evening.

"Why don't we split up into two groups to finish searching the drawers on this floor? That would cut that into half the time necessary," Mandie suggested.

"That's a good idea. We'll do that," Tommy said, giving the dumbwaiter a pull to send it down to the kitchen and then closing the panel over it.

With something else to look forward to, the group quickly finished searching the drawers on the third floor. They did not find a thing. Everyone met in the hall at the front of the house on the third floor.

"Now can we go to the attic?" Mandie asked, smiling up at Tommy.

Tommy looked around the group and asked, "Does everyone want to visit that smelly old attic?" He grinned at Mandie.

Everyone did, so he led the way through a narrow door at the end of the hallway and up steep steps to the room full of old treasures above. Pushing open the door, he reached inside and turned on the electric lights.

"Now, these lights are like what we have in our school," Celia said, looking at the wires suspended from the ceiling with a light bulb attached to the end hanging down.

Joe stooped to walk under one. "I wonder why they hung them so low you could bang your head on them," he said.

"They haven't really finished with these lights," Tommy said. "They are supposed to come back and put fixtures on the wall and do away with all this wire hanging down. In the meantime watch your head."

"Now, where is the collection you mentioned, Tommy?" Mandie asked, looking around the room. Everything was clean and neatly stacked and placed in position to be accessible.

"Over here," Tommy said, leading the way

across the huge room. He stopped at the far corner where there were all shapes and sizes of glass-doored cabinets filled with items from years long ago.

"Oh, how nice. I'm going to ask my mother to fix up our attic this way," Mandie said, moving along to look through the glass doors.

"The doors are all locked," Tommy told her. "That's to keep people from jumbling everything up or taking things out. You can see the various cards labeling the items. This collection was organized before I was ever born."

Mandie looked up at Tommy and asked, "Now, if that piece of hair in the library drawer came from here, how did anyone get it out?"

"Which cabinet did it come out of?" Celia asked.

Tommy quickly went down the rows and rows of cabinets and finally said, "I don't see a single vacant space where it could have been."

"Then maybe it didn't come out of any of these," Mandie said.

"Maybe it didn't," Tommy agreed. "But it looked similar to the other hair pieces in these." He waved his hand down the row.

Mandie had noticed that there were quite a few hair pieces in the cabinets. "Who would have access to the keys for the cabinets?" she asked.

"I suppose anyone who was able to get in my mother's private safe in my parents' room, and that person would have to know the combination, which even I don't know," Tommy explained.

"Are you going to mention this to your mother?" Celia asked.

"I don't think so, not right away," Tommy

replied. "There are so many things happening that could be upsetting."

"How about if we go downstairs and be lazy for a while in the parlor before supper?" Jonathan asked.

"Yes, we've had an awfully busy day," Robert quickly added.

"And I might possibly catch my grandmother alone to ask if she has decided what we can do about visiting Lily," Mandie told her friends.

"Let's go," Tommy said. He led the way down to the main floor and into the parlor.

"Oh, shucks!" Mandie exclaimed, looking around the room. "No one is in here."

"They are probably all in their rooms right now getting dressed to go out," Tommy told her.

"Yes, I suppose so," Mandie agreed as she sat down on a small settee.

"What are your plans for us tonight?" Jonathan asked Tommy as he sat beside him on another small settee.

"If everyone is not too tired, I thought we could go for a walk after supper when the air has cooled off," Tommy replied.

Everyone quickly agreed.

Mandie looked at Celia and secretly smiled at her. She knew Celia could read her mind and that she planned to walk past the Bedfords' house when they went out. She was determined to find out if the other girl in that house was actually Josephine. She had no idea as to how to find out, but she would think of some way to do it.

When the adults finally came into the parlor, they didn't even sit down but said good-night to the young people and left for their dinner out in town. Mrs. Taft was not alone, so Mandie could not approach her with any questions about anything, but she planned to accomplish that soon.

Chapter 8 / Where Did It Go?

Mandie and Celia were both sleepy and tired that night and didn't waste time getting ready for bed. Mandie pulled the counterpane down and upset Snowball, who was sleeping in the middle of it. He growled his displeasure and curled back up at the foot.

"I thought it was strange that there weren't any lights on in the Bedfords' house when we passed by tonight," Mandie said, crawling under the sheet.

"We were by early enough that someone should have been up," Celia said. She plumped up her pillow and relaxed.

"Maybe they were all out somewhere, but you'd think they'd at least leave a light burning," Mandie said. "We didn't solve anything today. All that searching of drawers and we didn't find anything. And we never even found out where those books came from in the bureau drawer because Tommy had never even seen them before."

"I wonder what we will do tomorrow," Celia mumbled, half asleep. "I forgot to ask Tommy if anything is planned."

"M-m-m," Mandie muttered. "Good night."

"Night," Celia answered.

And the next thing the two girls knew it was morning. The sun was shining brightly through the thin curtains. Snowball was sitting up in the middle of the bed washing his face and purring as he did it.

Mandie raised up on her elbow and said, "It must be time to get up." She rubbed her eyes.

"Yes," Celia agreed and tumbled out on her side of the bed.

Mandie threw back the thin sheet and slid to her feet, yawning and stretching as she looked around the room. "I wonder why no one came to wake us."

"I don't know, but I suppose we'd better hurry and go downstairs so we won't be late for breakfast," Celia said, rushing over to the wardrobe to pull down a dress.

"I don't think I even know what time breakfast is supposed to be," Mandie said, joining Celia at the wardrobe to get a dress.

Celia stopped by the mantelpiece to look at the clock. "Mandie, it's only five minutes to seven," she said.

"Five minutes to seven, but the sun looks like it is already high in the sky," Mandie said, glancing out the window. "I suppose that's because we are here near the ocean and not down between the mountains like we are at home." She quickly dressed.

"The boys are probably already downstairs," Celia said, fastening the buttons of her dress.

Mandie went over to the bureau to get her locket. She looked all over for it. It wasn't there. She became worried. "Celia, I can't find my locket," she said. "I know I put it here on the bureau last night when I took it off." She began moving everything around on the bureau. "Oh, where is it?" She was becoming frantic. Her locket contained the only picture she had of her father. It was made right before he died.

The bureau stood next to an open window. Celia hastily scanned the surface for the locket and then said, "Mandie, do you think it could have blown out the window?"

Mandie frowned and then laughed. "Oh, Celia, I don't think my locket could blow away. It's too heavy."

"But the winds are awfully strong here sometimes," Celia reminded her.

"I was awfully sleepy when I went to bed last night. Maybe I dropped it," Mandie said, getting down on her knees to look around the floor.

"Do you think Snowball could have jumped up on the bureau and played with it, maybe knocking it down on the floor?" Celia asked, also stooping to look around the carpet.

Mandie went back to the bed, pushed Snowball off, and shook the sheets and counterpane to see if the locket could have fallen there. She went to the wardrobe and examined the pockets of the skirt she had had on the day before, but they were empty.

"It just isn't anywhere," Mandie said, standing in the middle of the room and looking around.

"Are you sure you had it on when we came to our room last night?" Celia asked.

"Well, yes, pretty positive," Mandie replied. "I always take it off and put it on the bureau at night wherever I'm staying."

"But you don't wear it every day, do you?" Celia asked, standing up and straightening her long skirts.

"Almost every day," Mandie said. She looked around the room as she walked and said, "I've got to find my locket." She stood still to stomp her foot.

"Mandie, let's go downstairs and talk to the boys and see if they can offer us any advice," Celia suggested.

"All right, but I don't know how I can eat any breakfast until I find my locket," Mandie replied, going across the room to open the door. She looked back at Snowball, who had jumped back up onto the bed. "And I don't want to lose you, Snowball, so you just stay here, you hear?"

Snowball answered with a loud meow.

Mandie allowed Celia to go out first so she could be sure the door to their room was firmly closed. Then they walked down the long hallway to the main staircase.

All four boys were in the parlor, but no adults were in sight.

"Well, well, y'all are up bright and early," Tommy greeted them as he rose from the chair he was sitting in.

"It gets daylight here so early," Celia said, going to sit by Robert.

Mandie looked around the room and said, "If anyone finds a locket, I've lost mine,"

Joe came to her side and asked, "Do you mean the locket with your father's picture in it?"

"Yes, that's the only one I ever wear," Mandie replied, sinking down on a small settee, and Joe sat beside her.

Joe looked at the other boys and explained, "That locket contains the only picture Mandie has of her father, who died three years ago, as y'all probably know."

Jonathan came to kneel in front of Mandie and held her hand. "I'm sorry," he said. "We'll do our best to find it. It has to be somewhere."

"Thank you, Jonathan," Mandie replied. "It has to be in our room, but I can't find it."

Tommy came to sit in a nearby chair. "Mandie, do you think you could have lost it yesterday while we were at the Bedfords' house?" he asked. "Could it have fallen off? Remember Snowball's leash came unhooked. Maybe your locket also came unhooked."

"I don't think so, Tommy," Mandie replied. "I'm sure I had it on when we went to our room last night. Celia and I looked everywhere in the room and couldn't find it."

"Would you like for us to come and help you look?" Tommy asked, indicating himself, Joe, Jonathan, and Robert.

Mandie shrugged her shoulders and said, "I suppose it would be all right for you fellas to come and look if we leave the door open."

"Then let's do it," Joe told her as he stood up.

"Yes, right now, before we have to go in to breakfast," Tommy said.

They hurried to Mandie and Celia's room, and the first thing the boys did was jerk all the covers off the bed to be sure the locket was not between the sheets. Snowball protested and went racing about the room looking for another place to sit. It took only a few minutes for the four to search every inch of the room. The locket was nowhere to be found.

"It's definitely not in this room," Joe decided as they stood and looked about.

Cheechee had been attracted by the noise when she was going down the hallway, and she had stopped to watch and listen. Mandie saw her standing in the doorway and stepped over to explain. "We are looking for my locket, Cheechee," she explained. "Have you seen it?"

Cheechee shuffled her feet around and wouldn't look directly at Mandie. "De spirit in de night dun come and tuck it," she muttered.

"Now, Cheechee, you know I don't believe in ghosts and things like that, so please don't tell me some spirit came and got my locket," Mandie replied. "Did you see someone take it?"

"No, no, no," Cheechee quickly replied, violently shaking her head. "De spirit tuck it."

Mandie blew out her breath and looked at Tommy across the room. "Tommy, do you have spirits in this house?" she asked as she turned her back to Cheechee so the girl wouldn't see the grin on her face. "Cheechee says a spirit took my locket."

Tommy came across the room and looked at the young maid. "Cheechee, now what are you talking about? Do you know where her locket is? Tell us if you do." He smiled at her and added, "Please."

Cheechee looked down at the floor, shuffled her feet, and said, "I ain't seen no locket." She turned and rushed down the hallway.

Tommy turned back to Mandie and said, "I don't believe she knows anything about your locket, or she would have been bragging about it."

"I was hoping she did," Mandie said.

"I'm sorry, but I think we'd better get back downstairs. Everyone is probably ready for breakfast," Tommy replied.

Mandie shut Snowball up in her room, and all the young people went down to the parlor to join the adults for breakfast. All the time Mandie was wondering where her locket could be. She was confused now. Did she really have it on last night and leave it on the bureau? Or had she lost it during the day and not missed it? She couldn't figure out what to do next.

As they entered the parlor, Mandie spotted her grandmother sitting alone on the far side of the room. The other adults were carrying on conversations among one another. And the only one missing was Senator Morton, so evidently Mrs. Taft was waiting for him.

"Grandmother," Mandie said, rushing across the room before someone else joined her, "I have something to tell you." She quickly pulled up a stool next to Mrs. Taft's chair and sat down.

"Yes, what is it, dear?" Mrs. Taft asked. "What are you so upset about?"

Mandie smiled at her. Mrs. Taft seemed to be able to read her mind sometimes. "Grandmother, I've lost my locket with my father's picture in it," she explained. "We've searched our room, and it is definitely not in there. And now I don't know what to do next."

Mrs. Taft reached to pat Mandie's hand as she said, "Amanda, I've repeatedly told you that you need to take that picture out of the locket and have a photographer enlarge it enough to hang up. That way you would have two copies of the picture in case one got lost."

"I know, Grandmother, but I never seem to get everything done that I should. I'm sorry. If I can only find it this time I will give it to you to keep until I can get it done," Mandie replied, squeezing her grandmother's hand.

Senator Morton came into the parlor as Mandie looked up, and he headed straight for Mrs. Taft.

Mandie quickly glanced at her grandmother and asked, "Have you figured out how we could go visit Lily?"

By that time the senator was standing by Mrs. Taft's chair. He smiled down at Mandie and said, "I hear you heard from Miss Masterson, that nice young lady on the ship to Europe."

Mandie rose to go join her friends as she said, "Yes, sir, she and her little sister are back home in Fountain Inn."

"And you would like to visit them, of course," the senator said with a big smile. "Perhaps we can work something out."

Mandie grinned up at the tall, white-haired, distinguished-looking man and said, "Yes, sir, I would be most grateful if you could work something out so we could visit them."

"We'll see," Senator Morton replied, still smiling.

"Thank you, thank you," Mandie said and quickly went to join her friends as the adults were beginning to leave for the breakfast room. She had not thought of enlisting the senator's help in getting to visit Lily. Now that he was behind it, she was sure it would be accomplished.

When the young people had been seated at the breakfast table with their food, Tommy looked around the group and said, "I think I should say something to my mother to delay our visit to the beach house until we can find out if that is Josephine at the Bedfords' house. What do y'all think?"

Everyone nodded in agreement.

"Yes," Mandie said. "However, I don't know what you can say to your mother unless you tell her about the other girl at the Bedfords' house."

"I've been trying to think up something,"

Tommy said, looking around the group. "Does anyone have any ideas? I just don't want to tell my mother about our being at the Bedfords' house, not just yet. Believe me, it would be very unsettling if she found out about that."

"I could always say I just don't want to go to the beach house," Jonathan volunteered.

"I have a better idea," Joe said. "You could just tell her Mandie has lost her locket and we want to have time to look for it before we go to the beach house." He looked at Mandie and smiled.

Mandie smiled back and said, "Yes, I believe that would be a good excuse. It is the truth anyway. I'd rather find my locket before we move on to another house."

Tommy looked around the group and asked, "Is that acceptable to everyone?"

Everyone nodded in agreement.

"Then I will catch my mother after breakfast and speak to her," Tommy said. "I believe she was thinking of our going out there tomorrow."

"Thank you, Tommy," Mandie said. "I really do want to search for my locket, and I do hope I find it."

"And I hope you find it. We'll all be on the lookout to help," Tommy told her.

"I had a chance to speak to my grandmother before we came in here, and Senator Morton joined her and said he would be trying to find a way for us to visit Lily," Mandie told her friends.

"Don't count me in, because I will be leaving before the rest of you do to go home and spend some time with my parents before I go back to college," Joe reminded Mandie.

Robert looked across the table at Joe and said, "Perhaps we can get the same train, because I will also be going home before I return to school."

"Yes, that would be nice," Joe agreed.

Tommy looked back at Mandie and said, "Of course I won't be going with you to visit the girl. I've never met her anyhow. After all you people leave I will be going to Savannah to visit my grandmother for a few days."

Mandie looked at Tommy and said, "Now I suppose we will have to find out whether that is Josephine at the Bedfords' house or not so we can make plans for the rest of our visit here."

"Yes, and I would appreciate any suggestions anyone might have," Tommy told them.

"We could watch the house after dark. Then no one would see us," Jonathan suggested.

"I think we ought to just walk right up to the door and ask if your sister is there," Mandie said.

"But if that same man came to the door, you would never be able to make him understand what you want. Remember I told you he was a little foggy," Joe said.

"We could watch for someone else to come out of the house and ask them about Josephine," Celia said.

"Don't forget. Their gate is locked and you would have to jump the wall to get to the front door," Robert said.

"While we are doing all this thinking, please help me think up what to do next about my locket," Mandie reminded her friends.

"Yes, that is very important," Joe agreed.

"We need to retrace your movements yesterday," Tommy said. "And then search every place you've been."

"That will be quite a job, considering what all we did yesterday," Celia said.

"With all of us searching I hope we will find it," Tommy said.

Mandie looked at the adults at the other end of the table. They were beginning to get up. "I believe all the others are finished with breakfast," she said. "When are you going to speak to your mother, Tommy?"

Tommy quickly stood up and said, "I'll try right now." He hurried to join the adults as they began leaving the breakfast room.

Mandie watched as he caught up with his mother and walked with her out of the room as they talked. Then she looked around the table at her friends. "We had not even thought about the possibility that Mrs. Patton might want to go on to the beach house anyway," she said.

"Yes, she might," Joe agreed.

"In that case do you think we might be able to stay here while the adults go out there?" Mandie asked, looking around at her friends.

"I don't see why not," Jonathan spoke up. "We do things like that all the time at our house, some of the guests going different places and some staying home."

"But what about the servants?" Celia asked. "Do they take all the servants with them to the beach house?"

"I'm not sure," Robert said. "I've been here lots of times and we have all gone on to the beach house. I really don't know how many servants they have."

"As long as we had someone left here to cook for us we'd be all right," Mandie said.

"And they would probably insist that we have at least one adult here as a chaperone," Joe added.

"Here comes Tommy, and he doesn't look very happy," Jonathan said, looking across the room as Tommy came back to the table.

Tommy pulled out his chair and sat down. Looking around the table he said, "We almost lost that battle." He frowned and added, "My mother wanted to insist that we all go to the beach house tomorrow. She said that ought to give us enough time to find your locket, Mandie."

"And do we have to go then?" Mandie asked.

"No, I was able to win one day more to stay here, so we will have to go the day after tomorrow. My mother said that is final," Tommy explained.

"Does she have plans for us today and tomorrow?" Joe asked.

"No, the adults will go ahead with plans on their own, but we will have to be ready to move to the beach house the day after tomorrow, so we had better get busy and figure out what we are going to do about the Bedfords and also about searching for Mandie's locket," Tommy replied. "Let's go sit in the back parlor and formulate some kind of plan." He stood up.

As the group left the breakfast room Mandie had an idea. "I know that my grandmother is not too happy with hot beaches and that," she said. "I might be able to persuade her to stay here with us if we haven't yet solved the mystery of that other girl at the Bedfords' and have not found my locket."

Tommy looked down at her and said, "That's a good idea, Mandie. We'll see what happens."

Mandie was more worried about her locket than she was about who that girl at the Bedfords' might be. It was going to take some searching to find her locket. She wouldn't even think of the possibility of never finding the locket. She was determined to get it back.

Chapter 9 / Searching

"Today is Friday, so your mother expects us to move to the beach house on Sunday, then?" Mandie asked as the young people sat in the back parlor.

"Yes, it will be Sunday. I wonder if she has thought about that," Tommy said. "I'm sure we will all be going to church Sunday, and that won't leave much time after we eat and all that to get moved out to the beach house."

"What are we going to do about that second girl at the Bedfords'?" Jonathan asked. "Are we going to just walk up and knock on the door? Or what?" He looked around the room at the others.

"I suppose I should be the one who goes to the house, much as I hate to," Tommy said. "Because I'm not sure any of y'all could positively identify Josephine if she is at the Bedfords'."

"But if that is Josephine there and she gets a glimpse of you, she will quickly hide and you won't be able to find her," Mandie reminded him.

"You are right," Tommy agreed and looked around the room at the others. "What do y'all suggest?"

"She wouldn't know me," Jonathan said. "I've

never been here before. I could go to the door."

"But you wouldn't be able to identify Josephine, either," Mandie reminded him.

"Why don't we all go over the wall and surround the house?" Robert asked.

"Yes," Celia quickly agreed. "And we might be able to see through the windows whoever is in the house."

"When Jonathan and I went around the house before, most of the shutters were closed," Joe told them.

"Maybe we could go through a window and get into the house rather than knocking on the front door," Jonathan suggested.

"Oh no, Jonathan, they could press charges against us," Tommy quickly told him.

"Looks to me like the only way we can do it is just for everybody to walk up to the front door and knock," Joe decided.

"Yes," the others chorused.

Tommy stood up and said, "Let's go, then, before the sun gets too hot." He started for the door to the hall and stopped to say, "And let's go out the back door so we don't have to pass the parlor. My mother and the others are probably in there, and I don't want someone to ask where we're going."

"Good idea," Mandie said, following right behind him, and all her friends agreed.

When they got to the Bedfords' house they found the gate locked.

"Mandie, we can't just climb up there over the wall," Celia declared as the group stood there looking up at the wall.

"Yes, we can," Mandie told her.

Celia bent and tried to whisper to her, "But it would be indecent."

"Indecent?" Mandie loudly repeated and then covered her mouth as she saw the boys listening to them.

Joe grinned at Mandie and said, "Y'all just stay right here in the shade of that tree over there and we'll be right back."

"Oh, shucks!" Mandie said, stomping her foot.

"Come over in the shade, Mandie," Celia told her as she walked a couple of steps to the tree. "If only that gate was unlocked, we could follow the boys, but I think we'd better wait for them."

Mandie adjusted her straw hat brim so she could see the top of the wall as she joined Celia in the shade. She watched as the boys quickly went over the wall and disappeared into the overgrown front yard.

"I'm going back to the gate. Maybe I can hear what goes on in there," Mandie decided as she went back to attempt to see through the lacy ironwork of the gate.

She heard the knocker on the front door and knew the boys were finally knocking. Then there was a jumble of voices in low tones that she couldn't understand at all.

"Oh, why don't they talk loud enough for me to understand what they're saying?" she grumbled to herself.

She heard the door close and then there was silence. They must have all gone inside the house.

Celia came back over to join her. "Have you heard anything?" she asked.

"Just some mumbling and then the door closed," Mandie told her. She walked in circles in front of the gate as she became impatient for her friends to return. And she was beginning to feel the heat. Why were they taking so long? She could have been in and out of there half a dozen times by now. If only she had been able to get over the wall.

"Mandie, where are we going to look next for your locket?" Celia asked.

Mandie's attention immediately came back. "I suppose everywhere I've been since I came here," Mandie replied, looking down at the ground she was walking on. "Including around here." She began searching the ground as she moved around.

"This sand shifts so much when we walk on it, something could be just completely covered up with it," Celia said as she, too, looked around.

"Yes, and if I dropped my locket in sand like this I probably won't ever find it," Mandie said in a worried voice. She straightened up and looked at Celia. "But, Celia, I'm so sure I had it on last night. I've been thinking about what I did when I got ready for bed. I'm sure I can remember putting it on the bureau."

"If you did, then someone must have come into our room during the night and taken it," Celia decided.

"But who would do such a thing? And why didn't we hear them?" Mandie asked.

"I was awfully tired and went straight to sleep and didn't wake up all night," Celia said.

"I didn't wake up all night, either," Mandie said. She stopped to attempt to look through the gate. "These people really have everything grown up so you can't see into the yard, don't they?"

Celia joined her and put her face up near an open piece of ironwork. "Yes, and you know, I've been wondering whether they ever have anyone come to see them. If you tried knocking on this gate, no one in the house would hear you."

"I wonder who all lives in that big house, anyway," Mandie said, looking up where she could see the top of the mansion. "I certainly wouldn't like to live in a place all locked up like this one."

"Shh! Someone's in the yard," Celia whispered as she peered through a tiny opening in the ironwork.

Mandie moved up next to her. "I see someone," she whispered. "It's a girl, coming around the corner of the house." She reached to squeeze Celia's hand. "It's Josephine. It's Josephine."

"Josephine!" Celia whispered.

"She's coming this way," Mandie said, stepping back by the wall so the girl would not be able to see her.

Celia moved back with her, and they waited. Suddenly there was a click at the gate and the girls watched as it began to slowly move open.

Just as they started to move forward, Josephine saw them and quickly ran back into the yard, trying to slam the gate behind her, but it didn't shut.

"This way!" Mandie told Celia as she went through the gateway and followed Josephine around the house. "Hurry!"

But Josephine was too quick for them. She managed to open the door to the house, get inside, and slam it before they could get there.

"We can at least make some racket," Mandie said, beating on the door.

Celia stepped over to a window on the porch and began knocking on it. "Maybe the boys will hear us," she said.

"Joe was right. Josephine is here," Mandie said, pausing to rub her fists, which were beginning to feel bruised from the knocking.

"And she was probably coming out the gate to go home when we saw her," Celia added.

"Where are those boys?" Mandie moaned. "If they'd just come out right now they might be able to find her before she goes out the back door or somewhere else."

Finally the door opened, causing Mandie to almost fall inside as she raised her fist to knock. She looked up. It was Joe, followed by the other boys.

"Josephine is here," she quickly told them. "She came outside and was going through the gate when we caught up with her, but she ran back inside the house and shut the door," Mandie told him without taking a breath.

Joe quickly turned back into the house and the other boys followed him. Mandie and Celia stepped inside the huge foyer. Joe looked back and said, "Wait here." He hurried through a doorway, and Jonathan, Tommy, and Robert ran after him.

Mandie, afraid she would get lost in the big house or run into one of its occupants, stayed in the foyer with Celia. She could faintly hear the boys racing through the house, but no one came into the foyer.

In a few minutes they came back and Tommy said, "Maybe Josephine went home. I don't believe she's still in this house."

"Then let's go find out if she's home before she disappears again," Mandie said, going back to the front door.

As they all hurried back toward the Pattons' house, the boys tried to explain what they had found.

"The old man Joe saw was the grandfather and he's hard of hearing," Tommy explained. "He opened the door and let us in and couldn't understand what we wanted."

"And he insisted that we have coffee with him," Joe added.

"A manservant came down the hall with coffee and put it in the parlor," Jonathan explained.

"We heard someone talking in the next room, and when we went to see who it was they just vanished right quick," Robert said. "It was a girl, but it wasn't Josephine."

"That was Josephine we saw open the gate," Mandie said.

When they got to the Pattons' house, Tizzy informed them that all the adults had gone visiting somewhere and wouldn't return until afternoon.

"Did Josephine come home?" Tommy asked her as they all stood in the front hallway.

"No, ain't seen her at all," Tizzy said.

Tommy looked at his friends and said, "She could have come into the house without anyone seeing her. We can look in her room, but I doubt if she's there because she knows that's the first place we would go."

He was right. When they went upstairs to her room there was no sign of her.

"Let's just forget about Josephine for the time being," Tommy said as they went back down the hallway. "I'm tired of playing tricks with her. But we do know she is here and not at the beach, so I can tell my mother when she returns."

"Let's look for my locket," Mandie told him.

"Yes, we need to find your locket," Tommy agreed. "Now, let's think about where you've been in this house so we can search for it."

"We were all up on the third floor," Jonathan said. "Let's go up there and take a look from the widow's walk. We might see Josephine if she is in the yard."

"That's a good idea," Mandie agreed. Even though she didn't like the widow's walk, stuck high up there in the sky, she knew she should search for her locket on the third floor, and while they were at it they might as well look for Josephine, too.

Joe stayed right behind her going up the narrow steps to the roof. "Just don't look back," he told her. "I'm right behind you in case you slip."

"Thank you," she replied, finally stepping out onto the roof. Joe came along with her and held her hand.

Tommy walked around explaining what the sights were that they could see.

"We can see right down on other people's roofs," Jonathan remarked.

"Yes, and in some of the windows, too," Tommy said.

Mandie, holding tightly to Joe's hand, stopped to look at an open place in the distance. "Is that a park?" she asked. "Aren't those people playing music and dancing?" She could see quite a few people down there.

Tommy turned to look at her and replied, "That's a band of gypsies. They show up every now and then and stay a few days and then move on."

Mandie kept staring at the scene. "Real gypsies?" she repeated.

Tommy laughed, looked at her, and said, "Yes, real gypsies. Is there any other kind?"

Mandie looked at him and smiled back. "Come

to think of it, I suppose there isn't," she said.

They went back down to the third floor and began the search for Mandie's locket. It was a time-consuming job, and they finally stopped at noontime to freshen up and go downstairs for the noon meal, which Tizzy served in the breakfast room since the adults would not be present. Mandie brought Snow-ball down to the kitchen and Tizzy fed him.

As they sat at the table, Tommy sighed and said, "You know, all this detective work can really tire one out."

"It certainly can," Joe agreed with a grin at Mandie.

"That's because you don't enjoy it," Mandie said, smiling at them.

"I wonder where Josephine went," Celia said, taking a bite of potatoes.

"I wonder how she got to the Bedfords' when she was supposed to be at the beach with some friends," Tommy said, putting down his fork.

"That's nothing unusual for her," Robert remarked. "Nearly every time I've ever been here she has been missing or into something."

"Where do the people live that she was at the beach with?" Joe asked.

"They have a beach house not far from ours and my parents know them from a long time ago," Tommy explained. "They have a daughter about the same age as Josephine."

"Are you going to remind your parents that the day after tomorrow is Sunday, in case they don't want to move to the beach house on Sunday, like we discussed?" Mandie asked.

"Yes, as soon as they come home," Tommy said.

Before they had finished their meal they were surprised to see Mrs. Taft and Senator Morton return. Mandie looked up to see them standing in the doorway.

"Grandmother, are the others back, too?" Mandie asked.

Tommy rose to pull out some chairs. "Please come and join us," he told them. "Have y'all had anything to eat?"

"Yes, thank you, Tommy, we have eaten," Mrs. Taft said. "However, we will have coffee with y'all." She sat down across the table from Mandie.

The senator sat next to Mrs. Taft. "Yes, I could use a hot cup of coffee," he said.

Tizzy had followed them into the room and quickly set cups of coffee in front of them. She looked around the table and said, "If y'all ready fo' it, we still has some of dat chocolate cake." She smiled at Joe.

"Chocolate cake, that's wonderful," Joe replied with a big grin.

"Yes, bring on the chocolate cake," Jonathan added.

After Tizzy had served the cake and coffee, Mandie asked her grandmother, "Didn't y'all go with the others this morning when they went visiting?"

"Yes, we did, dear, but those were rather stuffy people and we thought we'd just come back and visit with y'all for a little while," Mrs. Taft said with a big smile.

"Stuffy people? That must be the Lesesnes you went to see," Tommy said, grinning.

"Exactly," Senator Morton replied as he smiled at the group.

"Another reason we came back early," Mrs. Taft

said, sipping her coffee, "I seem to have lost one of my diamond earbobs and I need to look for it."

"Your diamond earbobs?" Mandie repeated. She knew those earbobs must be worth a fortune, and also that her grandfather had given them to her grandmother when they were young.

"Yes, dear, and you're such a good detective I thought perhaps you could help us look for it," Mrs. Taft replied, smiling at Mandie.

"We've been looking for my locket. Remember I told you it was missing," Mandie replied.

"Yes, you did, and I certainly hope you find it," Mrs. Taft told her.

"We haven't found it yet," Mandie said.

"We've actually been looking for my sister, Josephine, too," Tommy told them. "She is supposed to be at the beach with friends, but here she turns up out at the Bedfords' house and we can't catch up with her."

"Oh dear, how did she get out there from the beach?" Senator Morton asked.

"That's what we want to find out," Tommy said. "When my mother comes home and catches up with Josephine, she'll straighten things out."

Mandie looked at her grandmother and said, "You know Tommy's mother wants us to all go to the beach house day after tomorrow and that's Sunday, and I wanted to stay here until I can find my locket. And since you have something missing that we need to look for, maybe you could stay here with us until we find my locket and your earbob."

"Of course, dear," Mrs. Taft replied. "I had already made up my mind that I wouldn't leave here until I find that earbob. The others can go ahead.

The senator and I will stay and help you find these things."

Mandie grinned and said, "Thank you, Grandmother."

"I'll ask my mother to leave Tizzy's sister, Mixie, here to cook for us until we join them at the beach," Tommy said.

"I knew everything would work out," Mandie said, smiling at Tommy.

"Now hold on a minute. My mother will have to agree to our plans," Tommy reminded her. "But since Mrs. Taft is involved I'm sure she will."

Mandie smiled and turned back to her grandmother. "Grandmother, would you like for us to search your room for the earbob?"

Mrs. Taft looked up from her coffee and said, "Why, yes, dear, that is a good idea. I tried looking for it, but I am not as young and nimble as you, so I'm sure you will do a more thorough job."

"We will," Mandie promised.

Mandie didn't want to discuss it in front of Tommy for fear he would be insulted, but she wondered if someone in the house had taken her locket and her grandmother's earbob. It was really strange that they both had jewelry missing. And then she wondered if anyone else had anything missing.

This was one mystery she definitely had to solve. It was important.

Chapter 10 / A Scary Discovery

As soon as the young people had finished their meal, Mrs. Taft told them, "Now, y'all go right ahead and look for my earbob in my room, or wherever, and I believe Senator Morton and I will just relax in the parlor. It has been a busy day." She rose from the table.

"We'll let you know when we finish," Mandie promised her as Mrs. Taft and Senator Morton left the room.

"Now, I suppose we have to get busy looking for that locket, too," Joe said as all the young people stood up.

"Maybe we'll find it and it won't take long," Mandie said, smiling at him as everyone left the breakfast room.

"If I remember correctly, your mystery solutions usually take a long time," Joe teased.

"But I have all this help this time," Mandie replied. As they continued down the hallway toward the main staircase, she suddenly stopped, stomped her foot, and said, "I had Grandmother right there where I could talk to her and I forgot to ask her if she had figured out how we could visit Lily. Oh, shucks."

"Well, if we hurry maybe she will still be in the parlor when we finish with her room," Joe replied.

"That's true because she won't be able to relax in her room while we are in it," Mandie said. "Yes, let's hurry."

They hurried through the search of Mrs. Taft's room as fast as they could, but it seemed that she had brought an awful lot of luggage. And the trunk was locked.

Mandie stood back and looked at the trunk. "I wonder what she has in there to cause her to lock it up," she said.

"Probably her expensive jewelry," Celia said.

"And maybe private papers," Jonathan added.

"Do you think her earbobs were in that trunk?" Mandie asked her friends. "She didn't say where they were supposed to be, did she?"

"We haven't seen a jewelry case, have we? So it's probably in that trunk," Celia surmised.

"Then the trunk must not have been locked all the time she's been here. How could anyone steal an earbob out of a locked trunk?" Mandie wondered.

"Now, just a minute, Mandie," Tommy quickly told her. "I don't believe your grandmother said someone *stole* her earbob, did she? As far as I remember, she said she couldn't find the other earbob."

"You are right, Tommy. I have a bad habit of assuming that whatever is missing that I am looking for has been stolen," Mandie answered. She looked around the room. "I believe we have finished. And the earbob is not in the room, unless it is in the trunk."

"I'd say we did a very thorough job," Robert said.

"Are you going down to the parlor and let your grandmother know that we have finished, just in case she is wanting to rest in her room awhile?" Celia asked.

"Yes, I suppose I should," Mandie replied as they went into the hall.

"While you go do that, Mandie, I think I will have a look around for my sister," Tommy said. "Anyone want to come with me?"

When all the others said they would, Mandie told them, "Maybe I can find out whether Grandmother has any plans yet about visiting Lily."

"Shall we meet back here in about thirty minutes, then?" Tommy asked. "Down in the alcove there." He pointed to where a group of chairs were placed at the far end of the hall.

"Yes, I'll be there," Mandie said, hurrying toward the main staircase as the others went in the opposite direction.

When she got to the front parlor, Mrs. Taft and Senator Morton were still there. She went across the room and pulled a stool near her grandmother and sat down.

"Grandmother, I'm sorry, but we couldn't find it," she told her. "Unless you have it in the trunk, which is locked, it is not in your room."

"No, it's not in the trunk. I've already checked inside it," Mrs. Taft replied. She frowned and said, "I don't understand how I lost just one of them. I put the set on my bureau last night and this morning one of them was missing."

"That is strange," Senator Morton said.

"But where is the one you didn't lose?" Mandie asked.

"Oh dear, I put it in the trunk immediately when

I discovered that one was missing, and I also locked up my jewelry case in the trunk," Mrs. Taft explained.

"Grandmother, I wouldn't say this to anyone else, but I believe someone stole my locket and your earbob," Mandie said and then waited for her grandmother's reaction.

Mrs. Taft looked around the parlor, lowered her voice, and said, "You know, dear, I have been thinking the same thing. They have quite a few servants here and they seem to move around all over the house."

Mandie looked at the senator and asked, "Senator Morton, have you missed anything personal?"

"No, Miss Amanda, I'm glad to say I haven't," he replied. "However, that may be because I always keep things locked up no matter where I am staying. I've traveled so much in my life I've just made that a habit."

"That is a good habit and if I can ever find my locket I'll never leave it out on a bureau again," Mandie said. "And, Grandmother, Tommy's sister, Josephine, was staying at the Bedfords' house and we saw her there."

Mrs. Taft quickly looked at Mandie and asked, "Now, when were you at the Bedfords' house?"

Mandie quickly explained about Snowball jumping over the wall and Joe rescuing him and seeing the girl he thought was Josephine. "So we went back this morning and found out it was Josephine. She started out the gate and saw us and went back into the house. But Tommy is sure she came home and is hiding from us somewhere in the house here."

"Have you told her mother about this?" Mrs. Taft asked.

"No, ma'am," Mandie replied. "Tommy wanted to be sure it was Josephine, and now that he knows he will speak to his mother when she comes home. I didn't tell Tommy, but I'm wondering if Josephine could be the one who took my locket and your earbob."

"Do you really think the girl might do such a thing?" Mrs. Taft asked.

"Yes, ma'am, she's a strange girl," Mandie replied.

"I'm terribly sorry about your locket, dear," Mrs. Taft said. "I know it can't be replaced. But I can get another earbob made to match the one I have left."

"I'm glad you can, Grandmother, because I know my grandfather gave those to you many years ago," Mandie said.

"If you think Josephine may have taken your locket, have you looked in her room for it?" Mrs. Taft asked.

"No, I haven't, Grandmother," Mandie replied. "If she took it I don't imagine she would leave it out where I could find it. And then, too, I haven't had a chance yet." She cleared her throat and asked, "What about Lily, Grandmother? Have you decided what we can do about visiting her?"

"No, Amanda, but I plan to inquire about the train route when I speak to the Pattons tonight," Mrs. Taft said, smiling at Mandie. "I'll let you know as soon as I can look into the possibility of visiting her, dear."

Mandie stood up and smiled back. "Thank you, Grandmother," she said. "I have to go back and meet my friends now. We are going to search my room for my locket again even though we've already done that. And we'll also be looking for Josephine."

"All right, dear," Mrs. Taft said. "If I happen to see that girl I will most certainly let you know."

"Thank you, Grandmother," Mandie said as she left the parlor.

She hurried down the hall to the stairs and went up to meet her friends. But when she got to the designated meeting place, no one was there. She walked around in circles, looking down each end of the hallway and going to the intersection of the cross hall, but the place seemed deserted.

"I wonder how long I've been gone," she mumbled to herself as she finally stopped and sat down on a chair where she could see if anyone was coming.

She waited and waited and no one came. Finally she decided to go to her room and get Snowball. He needed some fresh air and exercise. Maybe by the time she picked him up the others would have returned.

"At least my room isn't far away," she said to herself as she went down the other end of the hall and came to the door to her room.

Pushing open the door, she found Snowball curled up in the middle of the big bed. He opened his eyes, stood up, yawned, and stretched and purred loudly.

"Snowball, come on, let's go," she told him as she reached for his red leash on a nearby chair. He wanted to play and kept trying to roll over as she attached it.

"Be still, Snowball, if you want to get out of this room," she told him. "You aren't going anyplace without this leash."

Out of the corner of her eye Mandie suddenly saw something move past the half open door to the next room. She had not left that door open. She ran to push it back and look into the other room. She couldn't see anyone. But she was certain something had moved.

Snowball protested and tried to pull away from her. She quickly reached down and picked him up. He suddenly spit and growled. His fur stood up on his back. Mandie became frightened, but she made herself step into the other room and look around, holding Snowball tightly in her arms.

A door on the far side of the room seemed to be partly open. She went over to investigate and found it to be the doorway to an outside balcony. There was no one out there. She stepped back inside and pulled the door closed. Then hurriedly looking around the room, she went back into her room and firmly closed the door between them.

Snowball had relaxed and his fur was smoothed back down. Mandie stood in the middle of her room, thinking. Could that have been Josephine? Considering Snowball's reaction, it had to be someone he didn't like.

Then, remembering her friends, she went out into the hall, closing the door to her room, and hurried back to their meeting place. There was still no one there.

"Oh, where is everybody?" she mumbled to herself as she paced in circles, still holding Snowball. She shivered all over when she thought about that room next to hers. Who had been in there? And how did they get away so fast?

She looked down the hallway and saw Celia coming toward her from the other end. She hurried to meet her.

"Where have y'all been?" she asked.

"Chasing Josephine," Celia said, out of breath from walking so fast. "I told them I'd come and look for you because we were supposed to have already come back down here."

"Where are the boys? On the third floor?" Mandie asked.

"Yes, and we got a glimpse of Josephine in one of the rooms up there and then she disappeared," Celia explained.

"Come back to our room with me," Mandie said, walking in the other direction. Celia went along with her.

"I went in our room a while ago to get Snowball, and there is bound to have been someone in it," Mandie explained, pushing open the door to their room.

"Someone in our room?" Celia repeated as Mandie led the way in.

"This door over here," Mandie said, going over to the other door, "was partly open. I was putting on Snowball's leash and I got a glimpse of the door moving."

"Oh, Mandie, it couldn't have been Josephine because she is on the third floor," Celia said. "Who could it have been?"

"I don't know," Mandie said, pushing the door open. "I came in here and that other door there was open. There's a balcony outside it."

Celia stood there in the middle of the floor, looking at Mandie and then at the outside door. "Mandie, this is scary," she said. "I didn't know we had a door connecting to a room with an outside exit like this." She looked around. "Can we lock our door?" She went to examine the door.

Mandie said, "No, I've already looked and there

isn't a key in any of these doors. Remember Tommy said they never lock doors around here."

They stepped back into their room and Mandie closed the connecting door.

"I'm going to be afraid to sleep in here tonight," Celia said, rubbing her arms.

"But, Celia, who could it have been?" Mandie asked. "I was holding Snowball and he bristled up. That means it was someone he didn't like. Maybe Josephine?" She looked at her friend.

"No, Mandie, I just told you. Josephine is on the third floor. It couldn't have been her," Celia replied.

"I think there's a possibility it was her. She gets around awfully fast, you know. And she knows every crack and corner of this house. I know that from the last time I visited here," Mandie said.

"Come on, Mandie. I was supposed to come down here and get you," Celia said, walking over to the hall door and opening it.

Mandie followed her into the hall and firmly closed the door to their room. She put Snowball down and grasped the end of his leash.

"Snowball, you can walk for exercise, but you had better not try to run, you hear?" she said, straightening up to follow Celia.

"The boys are in the hallway by the door to the tower," Celia told her. "At least they were when I left. We should be able to find them somewhere around there."

"And where is Josephine?" Mandie asked.

"We saw her go in one of those rooms off that circular hall there, and Tommy says she has to come back out one of those doors because there is no other way," Celia explained.

"If he finally comes face-to-face with her, what

does he plan on doing?" Mandie asked. "She could still run away. Besides, what good will it do to catch up with her? I thought he only wanted to be sure she was in the house and was then going to tell his mother about her being at the Bedfords' house."

"I'm not sure," Celia said. "I know he wants to speak to her just for a moment, he said."

"Their mother is not home right now unless they came back after I left Grandmother in the parlor," Mandie said. "So Josephine could be long gone again before her parents return."

They found the boys where Celia had left them.

"Celia said you found Josephine," Mandie told Tommy.

"Yes, she's in there," he said, pointing to a closed door on his right. "And that's the only door out of that room."

"Why don't you just open the door and go in and talk to her?" Mandie asked, holding tightly to Snowball's leash as he prowled around.

"Because she would just run out and disappear somewhere again," Tommy said. "If I wait for her to come out, she can't get a head start on me and I'll just follow her and tell her a few things at the same time. And I'll also see where she goes and can tell my mother when she returns."

"I don't understand why she runs away all the time and won't listen to anyone," Mandie said.

"Her explanation for that has always been, 'No one listens to me and I'm not going to listen to you.' It's something she's made up to avoid behaving like she should," Tommy said.

"Did you ask your grandmother about visiting Lily?" Jonathan asked.

"Yes, and she is going to talk to my mother

tonight," Mandie said. "I think it all depends on whether the train goes through Fountain Inn or not."

"What did your grandmother say about the locked trunk?" Joe asked.

"She said she always keeps it locked wherever she goes because of business papers in it." Mandie hated lying to Tommy, but she didn't want to admit that she and her grandmother believed the house-keepers had something to do with the disappearing jewelry.

"Why don't y'all go help Mandie search her room again for the locket and I'll stay right here, at least for a while, and see if Josephine comes out," Tommy told the others.

"All right," Robert agreed.

"Yes, we can get that over with," Joe said.

As they started down the hallway, Tommy called to them, "Would someone please come and let me know if my mother comes home?"

"Yes," was chorused back.

Mandie let Snowball walk but she held firmly to the end of the leash. He tried to run ahead and then looked up at Mandie and fussed when he found he couldn't.

When they got to Mandie and Celia's room, Mandie stepped ahead to open the door. She went inside and quickly looked at the other door. It was still closed. She explained to the others about what had happened when she was in the room alone.

"Do you mean there's an outside door through there?" Joe asked, stepping over to open the door to the adjoining room.

"Yes," Mandie said, following him into the next room. She pointed to the outside door. "That one opens onto a balcony."

The boys went outside to look out from the balcony.

"I don't think anyone would be able to get up on that balcony from outside," Joe said, stepping back into the room. "It's a long way down to the ground and there aren't any steps that I can see."

"I plan on putting a big chair in front of our door tonight," Celia said.

Mandie looped Snowball's leash around the leg of a chair while they began searching every crack and corner of the room for her locket. She felt it was useless because they had already searched in here before.

And after a while when they finished she said, "Thank you all, but I didn't think we'd find it. I just feel that someone stole it because I know I put it on the bureau when I went to bed."

Everyone quickly looked at her. "But who would steal it?" Joe asked.

"No one in this household, of course, but since I found that outside door, I feel that somehow someone got in here from there and took it," she said.

Joe looked concerned and said, "Maybe Tommy can find a key to that door and lock it for you."

"Or maybe we could change rooms," Celia added.

"We can see what he has to say about it when we explain about that outside door," Mandie said.

She knew for sure that she was going to move all the furniture over in front of that adjoining room door tonight if no solution was worked out. And she doubted she would sleep a wink but would lie awake listening to every little sound all night long.

Chapter 11 / Plans Are Made

Just as Mandie and her friends were leaving her and Celia's room, Tommy came rushing down the hall to join them.

"Where's Josephine?" Mandie asked as she stepped back to allow Tommy to enter the room.

"She finally came out and of course she just ran away again," he replied. "I yelled at her that she had better not go off anywhere again, that I was going to tell our mother where she had been. She just ignored me and ran down the stairs back there. I'm tired of her so I just let her go."

"I want to show you something," Mandie said, picking up Snowball to carry him. She opened the door to the balcony and then looked at Tommy. "Did you know there is an outside balcony here? And none of these doors are locked and there are no keys in any of them?"

"Yes, I know about the balcony," Tommy said, looking beyond Mandie to the outside. Turning back to her he said, "But I told you we don't ever lock any doors. I've never even seen a key in a door that I can remember."

Mandie explained that she thought someone had

been in the adjoining room.

"It might have been Cheechee. You know she's always snooping around," Tommy said.

"I'm not sure it could have been Cheechee, because Snowball hissed and ruffled up his fur like he does when there's someone around that he doesn't like," Mandie replied.

"Tommy, can you find a key to lock the door to that other room there?" Celia asked, pointing to the adjoining room.

Tommy shook his head and said, "I can ask my mother about a key. I wouldn't know where to even look for one."

Joe looked at Jonathan and said, "Let's move a big chair in front of that door. Since it opens in this way that ought to hold it shut if someone tries to open it."

"Sure," Jonathan replied, stepping over to a large chair near the window. Joe joined him and they placed it in front of the door.

"Here, there's another chair," Tommy said. "We can move it over there, too." He and Robert picked up the other chair and set it beside the one Joe had moved.

Stepping back, Joe looked at the girls and asked, "Now do you think y'all will be all right?"

Mandie nodded and said, "If anyone tries to come through that door, at least the noise of pushing against those chairs will wake me."

"Those two chairs may deter an intruder, but, Tommy, I still wish you would ask your mother about a key," Celia said.

"I will," Tommy promised. "Let's go sit down for a little while." He led the way to the alcove at the end of the hallway where there were plenty of chairs for the group.

"What are we going to do about those old books in that bureau drawer?" Mandie asked as everyone sat down. She held Snowball in her lap.

"Do about those old books?" Tommy asked. "I suppose there's nothing to be done about those books. I don't know where they came from and I wouldn't know where to move them to."

"I just think it is a shame they are hidden away in that drawer when they seem to be such interesting books," Mandie said.

"If I have a chance I will ask my father about them," Tommy promised.

Jonathan cleared his throat loudly to get everyone's attention and said, "I think we ought to go down to the parlor. Who knows? There could be coffee and cake down there." He grinned at Mandie.

"You are probably right," Tommy said, rising from his chair. "We should go see."

When they got to the parlor, Tizzy was bringing in the tea cart for Mrs. Taft and Senator Morton, who were still there. Looking at the young people, she said, "I brought 'nuff fo' y'all, too. I figured y'all would smell dat coffee and be right heah after it." She smiled as she looked around the room.

"Thank you, Tizzy," Tommy said.

The others thanked the maid as she passed plates of chocolate cake and cups of hot coffee around.

Mandie went to sit near her grandmother as she took the plate and cup. "Grandmother, has my mother come back yet?" she asked.

"No, dear, none of them have returned yet," Mrs. Taft replied. "I'm glad you young people came to join the senator and me for cake and coffee. Did you not bring Josephine with you?"

Mandie knew her grandmother was trying to find out whether they had caught up with Josephine or not. She shook her head and said, "No, ma'am, she's upstairs." Then she added, "Somewhere."

Just as Tizzy was preparing to leave the room, Mandie heard the front door open and the sound of voices. Her mother and the others had returned. Tizzy also heard them and waited until they came into the parlor.

"We're just in time," Mrs. Patton said as she looked around the room. "Tizzy, do you have enough for all of us here?" She glanced at the tea cart.

"Won't take but a minute to go git mo', Miz Patton," Tizzy replied, going to wheel the tea cart out of the room.

As everyone came in and sat down, Mandie moved across the room to join her friends. The adults exchanged greetings with the young people and then carried on their own conversation.

During all the talking Mandie faintly heard her grandmother ask Mrs. Patton, "Do you know if the train will stop in Fountain Inn on our way back?"

That question caught the adults' attention and they stopped talking to listen.

"Yes, I believe it does stop there if there is someone who wants on or off as it goes through. Were you thinking of going to Fountain Inn?" Mrs. Patton asked.

"Well, yes, I was," Mrs. Taft replied, and then, turning to Elizabeth, she said, "Did you know Amanda received a letter from Lily Masterson saying she and her sister are back in Fountain Inn?"

Elizabeth smiled at her mother and said, "Yes, Mother, I saw the letter on the hall table when we came home from New York."

"Amanda and I would like to stop over in Fountain Inn and see her on our way back to Franklin," Mrs. Taft said.

"Just you and Amanda?" Elizabeth asked, looking across the room at Mandie.

"Well, Amanda and I and whoever else would like to join us," Mrs. Taft said, smiling at the young people who were listening to every word.

"I would, Mother," Celia told her mother.

"I knew you would," Jane Hamilton said, smiling at her daughter. "We'll see what we can work out."

"Please include me," Jonathan said, glancing at his father across the room.

"And of course Senator Morton," Mrs. Taft said, turning to look at him. He nodded.

"I believe we are going to have to work out a plan here," John Shaw said.

"Definitely," Mr. Guyer agreed.

It took an hour to do it, but the adults finally came to an agreement.

"Now, you will only stay over one night to visit Lily," Elizabeth told Mandie.

"Yes, ma'am," Mandie replied with a big grin, happy that she would be able to visit her friend.

"And the rest of us will go back to Franklin," Mr. Guyer told his son. "I can wait one day for you to come back and join me to go home to New York and no longer. Is that understood?"

"Yes, sir, thank you," Jonathan replied.

"What about you, Joe?" John Shaw asked. "Are you stopping over with them, or are you going home early?"

"I don't know exactly how long y'all will be staying here, but I will leave next Tuesday and go home so I can spend some time with my parents before I return to college, sir," Joe replied.

"And I will be getting the train with Joe. I have to get back and visit other relatives," Robert added.

"Then I believe we have everything settled," John Shaw said.

After they finished the coffee and cake, everyone went to their rooms to relax and freshen up for the evening meal.

Mandie was excited about the prospect of seeing Lily and Violet Masterson. She and Celia sat in their room and discussed it for a while. Then Mandie decided she should take Snowball down to the kitchen and leave him so Tizzy could feed him.

"I won't be gone but a minute," Mandie told Celia as she picked up the white cat.

Celia followed her to the door. "I'll go with you," she said.

Mandie stopped and looked at her. "We forgot to ask Mrs. Patton about a key to that door," she said.

"That's why I'm going with you," Celia said. "I'm not staying in this room by myself."

"All right, let's go," Mandie replied, going out into the hall. Celia followed.

They found Cheechee in the kitchen, and she immediately took over Snowball.

"Will you please be sure he gets something to eat, Cheechee?" Mandie asked.

Cheechee never had much to say. She nodded her head and took Snowball over to the sandbox in the corner. Tizzy came into the room then. "I knows dat white cat be hungry now," she said. "Don't you go and worry 'bout him. We'se gwine feed him good."

"Thank you, Tizzy," Mandie said. "I'll get him later."

"No need, missy," Tizzy said. "After he eats I'll take him back to yo' room."

"Thank you, Tizzy," Mandie said.

She and Celia went back down the hall and up the stairs to their room. Just as they came around the corner from the cross hall, Mandie looked ahead. Josephine was coming out of their room. She raced ahead.

"Josephine!" Mandie said, stopping in front of her. "What were you doing in my room?"

Josephine frowned at her and said, "Not your room. The room belongs to the house and the house is mine." She started to move on.

Mandie stepped back and got in her way. "You took my locket off my bureau, didn't you? And Grandmother's diamond earbob? Didn't you? Admit it," she angrily accused the girl.

Josephine looked at her with her mouth open and said, "What would I want with that old locket of yours? Cheap thing? And I sure don't wear diamond earbobs." She started to move around Mandie.

Mandie kept stepping in her way. "I'm going to tell your mother that you took my locket and Grandmother's earbob," she said.

Josephine stopped and raised her hand as though to slap Mandie, but Mandie dodged. "And if you do you'll be telling a lie," she said and raced down the hallway.

"Come on, Mandie, let's go into our room," Celia said.

Mandie looked at the girl running down the

corridor and then turned to enter the room with Celia. She plopped down in one of the big chairs. "She took them," she said. "I've felt all the time she did."

"But, Mandie, you don't have any proof of it," Celia reminded her as she sat in the other chair.

"She has never liked me and she's always up to some mischief or other," Mandie replied.

"I don't believe she likes anyone," Celia said.

"I'm going to search her room as soon as I get a chance," Mandie decided.

"I'm going to change clothes," Celia said, rising from her chair.

"And I am, too," Mandie said.

"We don't have much time," Celia said, glancing at the clock on the mantelpiece.

"I know," Mandie said, finally getting up to go to the wardrobe for another dress.

While they were changing clothes there was a knock on their door. Mandie quickly buttoned her dress and went to answer it.

Joe was standing outside, smiling. "Guess who is here?" he asked.

Mandie looked at him and couldn't imagine who he was talking about.

"Uncle Ned," Joe said with a big grin. "He's in the parlor when y'all get ready to go down." He turned back down the hallway.

"Tell him I'll be down shortly," Mandie said excitedly.

"So Uncle Ned is here," Celia said as Mandie turned back into the room.

"Yes, you know he always checks up on me wherever I go," Mandie said and then added sadly, "because he promised my father he would look after me when he died." She hurried over to the bureau to brush her hair.

"I know," Celia said, tying a ribbon in her hair. "I wish my father had had a friend like him when he died."

Uncle Ned was not related to Mandie. He had been a lifetime Cherokee friend of her father's and had helped her find her real Cherokee kinpeople. She had not known until Uncle Ned told her that her father was one-half Cherokee.

"Uncle Ned is your friend, too, Celia," Mandie reminded her. "I do believe he loves you as much as he does me. He's like a grandfather to both of us."

"Yes," Celia agreed. "I'm glad he came because I know you must want to discuss all the happenings here with him."

"I plan to as soon as I can get a chance," Mandie agreed.

They went down to the parlor and found Uncle Ned and all the boys there.

Mandie hurried across the room to embrace the old man. "How long are you going to be here, Uncle Ned?" she asked as he rose from his chair.

The old Indian looked down at her and said, "Not long. Need talk with John Shaw." He seemed worried.

Mandie looked up at him and asked, "Is something wrong?"

At that moment John Shaw came into the parlor. Crossing the room to shake hands with Uncle Ned, he said, "I'm glad you came down here to join us, Uncle Ned."

The two men sat down and the young people listened to their conversation.

"Not good news, John Shaw," Uncle Ned began, glancing at Mandie.

"You have bad news, Uncle Ned?" John Shaw quickly asked.

"Trouble back home," Uncle Ned explained. "Find trouble in secret tunnel in John Shaw's house."

Knowing she should not interrupt, Mandie was anxiously listening. Trouble in the secret tunnel? What could it be?

"In the tunnel, Uncle Ned," John Shaw said. He frowned as he asked, "What kind of trouble?"

Uncle Ned was always slow and thoughtful when explaining anything. He said, "Abraham find crack in wall in tunnel, big crack."

Everyone took a deep breath as they listened.

"A crack?" Mandie asked.

John Shaw looked at the old man and quickly asked, "A crack? What seems to be the problem? Do you have any idea as to what caused it?"

Uncle Ned quickly nodded his head and answered, "Tornado, must be tornado made crack, shook house."

A tornado had passed through Franklin, North Carolina, a few weeks ago while Mandie and her friends were home for spring holidays.

"Uncle Ned, is it serious? Is it a large crack?" John Shaw quickly asked, leaning forward and frowning in deep concern.

Uncle Ned nodded. "Must see. Must fix," he replied.

John Shaw took a deep breath, rose from his chair, and paced about the room. "Then I suppose we had better go home at once," he told the old man. "I just hope it is not serious."

Mandie and her friends listened to the conversation and looked at each other.

"Do all of us need to go home, Uncle John?" Mandie asked.

John Shaw stopped to look at her and replied, "Yes, I think that would be the best way. We'll all go at once as soon as we can get the train."

Then Mandie remembered Lily. She, Celia, Jonathan, Mrs. Taft, and the senator were supposed to stop off on the way and visit Lily. She quickly decided their plans would have to be cancelled. This situation seemed to be urgent, and besides, she wanted to get home and see for herself what was happening to their house.

All her friends immediately agreed it would be best if they all left together.

"We won't be able to get the train until tomorrow," John Shaw told Uncle Ned. "Did you come on the train?"

"Yes," Uncle Ned replied. "I go back with you on train tomorrow."

"I'll have to speak to Lindall Guyer. We came in his private car on the railroad," John Shaw said.

Mandie and her friends looked at each other and Mandie said, "Tommy, I hope you don't mind if we go home earlier than we planned. And, Joe, will you be going with us rather than waiting until next week to leave here?"

"Of course I understand, Mandie," Tommy replied.

Joe ran his long figures through his unruly brown hair and said, "I suppose I might as well go on with y'all. That would give me a little more time with my parents before I return to college."

"I hope y'all don't mind, but I will stay on here

until next week, as I had planned," Robert told them.

Celia quickly looked at him and asked, "You don't want to go when we go?"

Robert smiled at her and replied, "I wouldn't be any help in repairing a crack in the bottom of a house, so I'll just stay here a few more days in the nice beach weather with the Pattons when they go out there. Maybe I'll see you again before school starts back."

"That would be nice," Celia said with a shy smile. "Right now I don't know where my mother and I will be, but I'm sure we will go home with Mandie tomorrow."

"I'll find out," Robert promised.

Mandie wanted a chance to speak privately with Uncle Ned about the mysteries occurring in the Patton house. She wanted to get away from her friends to do this. Later that night after supper she finally got her chance to ask him if they could go for a walk and talk.

"Too late to walk tonight," Uncle Ned told her. "Early tomorrow morning we walk, talk, before train comes."

Mandie smiled up at him and agreed. "All right, Uncle Ned, I'll meet you down here before breakfast."

Mandie was tired from all the events and planning that had taken place. She was glad when she and Celia finally went to their room for the night.

"I'm plumb tuckered out," Mandie said, pushing open the door to their room. She plopped down in a chair nearby.

"Me too," Celia agreed, going over to the wardrobe. "But I think I'll get ready for bed before I relax."

"Yes, and I should, too," Mandie said, joining her.

After they had put on their nightclothes they decided to get in bed. Mandie shook Snowball off the counterpane and turned down the covers. The white cat curled up at the foot of the bed.

And once they were in bed they both dropped off to sleep.

Mandie was awakened by Snowball growling and hissing in her ear. She reached up to smack him and then came wide awake because his fur was ruffled up and he was acting strange. She raised up on her elbow and suddenly saw something shadowy moving by the chairs. She quickly pinched Celia.

Celia woke and before she could speak Mandie reached for her hand. That was always their signal for repeating their Bible verse.

" 'What time I am afraid, I will trust in thee,' " they said together.

Mandie tried to see through the darkness. Whatever had been in the room with them seemed to have suddenly vanished. She shakily reached for the lamp switch by the bed. When the light came on there was no one there.

"I know there was someone in this room," Mandie whispered, sitting up. "Snowball was acting like he did earlier today, hissing, and he woke me up."

Celia sat up and looked around. "I don't see anyone, Mandie."

Mandie looked at her cat. He had become quiet and was washing his face as he sat in the middle of the bed.

"There is something strange about this room," Mandie declared. "And I'm going to leave the light on for the rest of the night."

Celia pulled the covers around her shoulders and

said, "Yes, leave the light on."

"I wonder if Josephine could have been in this room just now," Mandie said.

"She never did show up for supper," Celia reminded her.

"I noticed that, but she is friends with Cheechee and I'm sure Cheechee took her something to eat in her room. I would like to have a chance to search her room before we leave to go home."

"If she took your locket, Mandie, she probably put it someplace where you would never find it."

"She's so unreasonable in everything she does that you never know what she's up to next," Mandie said.

Celia dropped off to sleep. Mandie stayed awake for a long time thinking about everything that had happened since they had arrived at the Pattons' house. She needed to discuss this with someone and she was glad Uncle Ned had arrived. He was always ready to listen with advice.

Chapter 12 / The Thief

The next morning Uncle Ned was waiting for Mandie when she brought Snowball and came down to the kitchen. Tizzy was already there and had a pot of coffee made. She brought a cup to the table for Mandie to sit with Uncle Ned, who had just started drinking his. Snowball ran to a plate of food that Tizzy placed on the floor by the huge cookstove.

"Thank you, Tizzy," Mandie said as she sat down.

"Must hurry," the old man reminded her as he sipped his coffee.

Mandie took her spoon and began dipping it in and out of the coffee in an effort to cool it down enough to drink. "I know, Uncle Ned. I don't really want this whole cup of coffee, so I'll be ready whenever you are to take a walk outside," she replied.

Mandie didn't want to begin a discussion with Uncle Ned with Tizzy present to hear, so she hurriedly drank a little of the coffee, and as soon as Uncle Ned finished his, she said, "I'm ready." She rose from the table and reached for Snowball's leash, which she had hung on the back of a chair. "I want to take Snowball with us. He needs to walk."

She quickly stooped down to fasten the cat's leash to his collar as he finished his food.

"Let's walk toward the water," Mandie suggested once they were out in the yard.

"Yes," the old man agreed.

As they walked, Mandie began relating the events that had taken place since they had come to the Pattons' house. When they got near the water they sat on a low wall and Mandie tied Snowball's leash around an iron stake nearby. He protested and tried to get loose.

"Uncle Ned, my locket was missing when I got up the other morning and Grandmother's diamond earbob was, too, and we've searched everywhere and can't find them," Mandie told him. "However, I know that Josephine must have taken them. I told her so and she got furious with me." She stopped and frowned.

"Must not judge unless know," the old man quickly told her. "Remember, think before act." He looked worried.

"But I know that she must have taken them," Mandie insisted.

"How know? See her take?" Uncle Ned asked.

Mandie looked up at him and said, "I didn't actually see her take them, but she has acted strange the whole time we've been here and she doesn't like me."

"Must not accuse without proof. I tell Papoose before, never judge without proof," Uncle Ned said firmly. "Must do what Big Book says, judge not." He frowned as he looked at her.

Mandie felt her temper flaring up and tried to control it but didn't succeed very well. "Oh, Uncle Ned, I just know Josephine took my locket and my grandmother's earbob. There's no one else who could have done it," she insisted.

Uncle Ned shook his head and said, "Must not accuse, not see. Not right to do that. Must ask her forgiveness."

"Never will I ask Josephine's forgiveness for anything," Mandie quickly replied, stomping her foot in the sand. "She needs to ask mine."

"Big Book say forgive," the old man said.

Mandie jumped up and pulled on Snowball's leash as she unhooked it. He protested by rolling over in the sand. "I have to go back now, Uncle Ned," she said, trying to keep her voice from shaking. "I have to get my things packed for the train." Uncle Ned was wrong this time. That girl had stolen the locket and the earbob, she was sure. No use arguing about it.

Uncle Ned rose and said, "Yes, we go."

They silently walked back to the Pattons' house. Mandie was angry with the old man, and she could tell he was angry with her. There was no use in trying to discuss this with him. Snowball tried to run ahead. She held tightly to his leash.

At the house, Mandie quickly entered the front door and, without looking back at him, she said, "I'm going up to my room now."

"Think, Papoose, think," the old man told her as she picked up Snowball and rushed ahead for the staircase.

When she got to the top of the steps, she slowed down to take a deep breath. Snowball tried to wriggle loose, but she held him tightly.

When Mandie opened the door to her and Celia's room, Snowball hissed and bristled up as he managed to escape from her arms. He raced across the room toward the bureau. Mandie stopped in shock as she watched him jump up onto the bureau to chase what looked like a real live monkey sitting there holding Celia's red ribbon. The animal responded in his own language to the cat's growl and quickly leaped through the open window, taking Celia's ribbon with him. Snowball didn't slow down as he continued the chase.

Mandie ran over to the window to grab the cat, but he managed to go through right after the animal. She leaned over to look outside. The balcony by the room next door extended to the edge of her window and both animals had jumped onto it. The monkey dropped Celia's ribbon in one of the huge flowerpots sitting on the balcony and then rushed over the edge. Snowball jumped up after him and sat on the balcony rail and growled.

Without thinking of the danger, Mandie slipped through the open window and jumped down to the balcony, trying to rescue her cat.

"Snowball, come here," she demanded as the cat sat on the edge looking down after the monkey, who had disappeared from her sight.

She carefully moved over to reach Snowball when she noticed the red ribbon in the flowerpot. Stopping to pull it out of the sticky plant, she suddenly saw something shiny in the sunshine on the dirt in the pot. Reaching between the sharp leaves, she pulled it out. When she saw what it was, she sat down on the balcony floor and started crying as she held it tightly. It was her locket. Snowball turned back to see what was wrong with his mistress. He jumped down and came to try to sit on her lap.

"Oh, Snowball, it's my locket," Mandie cried, opening the locket to be sure her father's picture was still inside. She gazed into his beloved face and tears streamed down onto her cat.

Celia suddenly appeared in the window to their room. "Mandie, what are you doing down there?" she asked leaning out to look.

Mandie held up the locket and couldn't speak because of tears as she stood.

"You found it!" Celia excitedly called to her.

Mandie nodded and looked around for a way to get back up through the window in their room.

"Wait," Celia told her. "I'll get one of the boys to help you back up. Wait right there." She disappeared from the window.

Mandie wiped her eyes on the hem of her long skirt and stepped over to the flowerpot to get Celia's red ribbon. And she again saw something shiny. Reaching into the pot she pulled it out. It was Mrs. Taft's diamond earbob.

"Grandmother, I've found it for you," Mandie muttered to herself as she rubbed the dirt off the earbob.

Then she suddenly wondered where the monkey had gone. Going to lean over the edge of the balcony, she saw a small boy in brightly colored clothes standing in the yard below. The monkey was making its way down the steep outside steps toward him. "The gypsies," Mandie said to herself. She wondered if the gypsies had taught that monkey to steal.

"Mandie!" She heard her name and looked up to see Joe climbing out of the window. "I'm coming down to get you." He jumped down and asked, "Mandie, how did you get down here?"

"The way you just did, Joe, and look here," she said, holding up her locket and her grandmother's earbob. Pointing over the edge of the balcony, she added, "The monkey down there stole them."

Together they looked over the edge. The monkey had made it down to the ground, and the little boy picked him up as he looked up at Mandie and Joe.

"Go home," Joe yelled at the boy.

Tommy appeared in the window and jumped down to join them. "Get going," he yelled at the boy below. "Right now, you hear? Go home."

The gypsy boy finally turned and started to walk away, carrying the monkey with him.

It took the help of both boys to get Mandie back into her room. She couldn't reach the windowsill. Joe boosted her up so that Tommy could stand in the window and get hold of her hands and pull her through into the room. Mandie collapsed on the floor as Joe sent Snowball through behind her.

Tommy knelt by her side and asked, "What happened? Why were you down there on that balcony?"

Joe stepped through the window into the room and bent to look at Mandie as he asked, "Are you all right?"

Celia reached and took her red ribbon that Mandie held out to her.

"I've never been so scared and so happy all at the same time," Mandie finally replied as she saw Jonathan and Robert come into the room. She showed everyone her locket and the earbob as she stood and shook her skirt. "I need to get cleaned up," she added.

"We'll wait for you on the landing of the main staircase," Joe said as all the boys left the room.

"Mandie, I'm so happy you found your locket," Celia said. "And I'm glad it wasn't Josephine who took it and your grandmother's earbob."

Mandie turned around to look at her and said, "Oh, Celia, I accused Josephine of taking them." And she also remembered arguing with Uncle Ned about it just a little while ago.

"I know," Celia replied, sitting on the bed. Snowball jumped up beside her and began washing his face.

"Celia, I've got to find Uncle Ned right away," Mandie said. "Just as soon as I get cleaned up."

The girls securely closed the window in their room, left Snowball on the bed, and went to meet the boys.

"I have to find Uncle Ned right away," Mandie told the boys. "I'll find y'all later."

"We'll be in the back parlor," Tommy told her.

Mandie held the locket and the earbob tightly in her hand as she hurried down the stairs and to the main parlor. There was no one there and no one in the hallway. She opened the front door. Mrs. Taft was walking about the yard with Senator Morton.

"Grandmother!" she called excitedly as she ran to her. She held out the earbob and her locket in her hand. "Look! I found them!"

"Where?" Mrs. Taft asked with a big smile as she took the earbob.

"Let's sit down on that bench over there and I'll explain."

As soon as they were seated beneath the palm tree, Mandie explained what had happened. She added, "And, Grandmother, I would like for you to lock up my locket in your jewelry case, please. I am not going to wear it anymore until I get the picture enlarged like you've always told me to."

Mrs. Taft took the locket and smiled at her. "I am so happy that these have been found. I'll go up to my room right now and lock them up where they'll be safe." She stood up.

Mandie rose, too, and said, "I need to find Uncle Ned. Have you seen him?"

"I believe he was in the barn with the other men looking after the horses just a little while ago," Senator Morton said.

"Thank you, Senator Morton, I'll go see," Mandie called back as she raced down the pathway to the back of the house.

She dreaded facing Uncle Ned and admitting she had been wrong about Josephine, but it had to be done, and the sooner the better to get it off her mind.

Uncle Ned came out of the barn as she got within sight of it, and he was alone. "Uncle Ned," she called to him as she hurried on. "Wait for me."

The old man stopped and looked at her. Mandie hurried up to his side and took his hand in hers as she said, "Uncle Ned, I am sorry. I was wrong about Josephine." She quickly explained about the monkey and then looked up at him as she asked, "Will you please forgive me? I'm sorry." Her voice choked up and she couldn't say another word.

Uncle Ned looked down at her, squeezed her hand, and said, "Yes, I forgive Papoose."

"Thank you, Uncle Ned," she said.

"Now Papoose must ask Josephine forgiveness," he said. "And must always stop to think before act."

"I know, Uncle Ned, and as soon as I can find Josephine I'll apologize," she said.

"Must hurry," the old man said. "Get train two hours."

"Two hours?" Mandie asked. "I have to pack my things, too."

Mandie went back inside the house to look for the girl, which was going to be an endless task, as Josephine always managed to disappear. Going up the main staircase, she kept watching for Josephine, but she was nowhere around. When she reached the hallway where her room was, she was amazed to see the girl coming out of her and Celia's room. She felt her anger rise. She took a deep breath and hurried forward. Josephine stopped to look at her.

"Josephine, I want you to know that I'm sorry I accused you of taking my locket and Grandmother's earbob, because I found them. The gypsies' monkey has been coming through the window in our room and I saw him today. I found the locket and earbob in a flowerpot on the balcony where he dropped Celia's red ribbon. I'm sorry." Mandie waited for a reply.

Josephine stood absolutely still for a moment and then she said, "I would like to play with your cat."

Mandie was always amazed by reactions from the girl. Her apology seemed to have floated off into air, without Josephine even acknowledging it. Then Mandie realized Josephine must have been going into their room to play with Snowball.

Smiling, Mandie said, "You may play with Snowball any time you like, Josephine, but please don't let him get outside."

Josephine looked at her, pushed the door back open, and went inside.

Mandie hurried back downstairs to join her friends. They were in the back parlor.

"I left Josephine playing with Snowball in our room," she said to Celia.

Everyone looked at her in surprise.

"It seems that must be the reason she has been going in our room, just to play with Snowball," Mandie said.

"What did you do with your locket?" Joe asked.

"I gave it to Grandmother to lock up in her jewelry case for me," Mandie replied.

"I'm certainly glad we've got that all settled," Tommy said.

"I have to pack my trunk because we are leaving in two hours, in case no one has told you," Mandie said. "But first I'd like to go outside and see if that little boy really left."

Her friends already knew they had two hours to get ready to leave for the train.

"Your Uncle John came and told us," Celia explained.

"Come on if we are going outside," Joe said. "We don't have much time."

They went out the front door and walked around to the outside staircase.

Mandie looked up but there was no sign of the monkey or the boy. Then she thought she saw something on a step above.

"Do you see something up there?" she asked her friends.

Tommy squinted his eyes and said, "I do believe there is something up there. I'll go see." He hurried up the steep steps.

The others watched as he stooped and picked up something.

"Someone's handkerchief," Tommy said, holding up a lacy square of linen as he came back down.

"Oh, that's mine," Mandie said, reaching out to take it. "I must have lost it while I was on the balcony." She remembered that she had reached in the pocket of her skirt for her handkerchief and it was not there. She had rubbed her eyes on the hem of her skirt.

"Let's get our things packed," Jonathan reminded the others as he led the way back into the house. "My father's railroad car is ready."

"Yes, let's hurry. The sooner we get back to my house and find out what is wrong, the better," Mandie said as she rushed behind him, and the others followed.

Mandie was anxious to go home because she was also anxious to leave the Pattons and Josephine, especially, while nothing else was happening. Their visit to Charleston had had too many problems this time.

Then she began thinking of the crack in the secret tunnel at home. Had the tornado caused it? And what could be done about it? It all sounded like a big mystery to her. She could hardly wait to get home to solve it.

Mandie was sorry to miss seeing Lily Masterson on her way back to Franklin. Maybe she would be able to persuade her grandmother to make the journey back down on the train one day soon for a visit.

However, the crack in the secret tunnel was more important.

COMING NEXT!

MANDIE AND THE HIDDEN PAST
(Mandie Book/38)

An old, old mystery is solved.

MANDIE® Books

from Lois Gladys Leppard and Bethany House Publishers

At the turn of the nineteenth-century, Mandie Shaw is about to become a teenager. Living in the back woods of North Carolina, she soon finds herself involved in mysteries, adventures...and fun! Joining Mandie are her new friends, including Celia, Joe, Molly, Jonathan, and, of course, her lovable kitten, Snowball. Each Mandie book is a journey into a world of excitement and a peek into the life of someone very much like you!

MANDIE and...

⚜ BETHANYHOUSE

11400 Hampshire Ave. South, Minneapolis MN 55438 • www.bethanyhouse.com